Smile Time Books are written for anyone who enjoys a feel-good story, and their short chapters make them ideal for reading to children at bedtime.

I0596253

Other books by Robert Kingsley Hawes

The Girl I the Yellow Hat
The Jetty War

The Magpie Way (book 1)
Finding Alice

The Magpie Way (book 2)
The Great River

When Pop Took Us Fishing

A DOG ON THE RUN

This story was inspired by two amazing friends who were brought together by a strange twist of fate. Their real-life meeting is told in verse at the back of this book.

Robert Kingsley Hawes

Published by Smile Time

ISBN 978-0-6452189-0-9 (paperback)

First edition, 2021

For book orders and enquiries, contact: r.hawes70@gmail.com

A catalogue record for this book is available from the National Library of Australia

CONTENTS

MacLeod's Farm

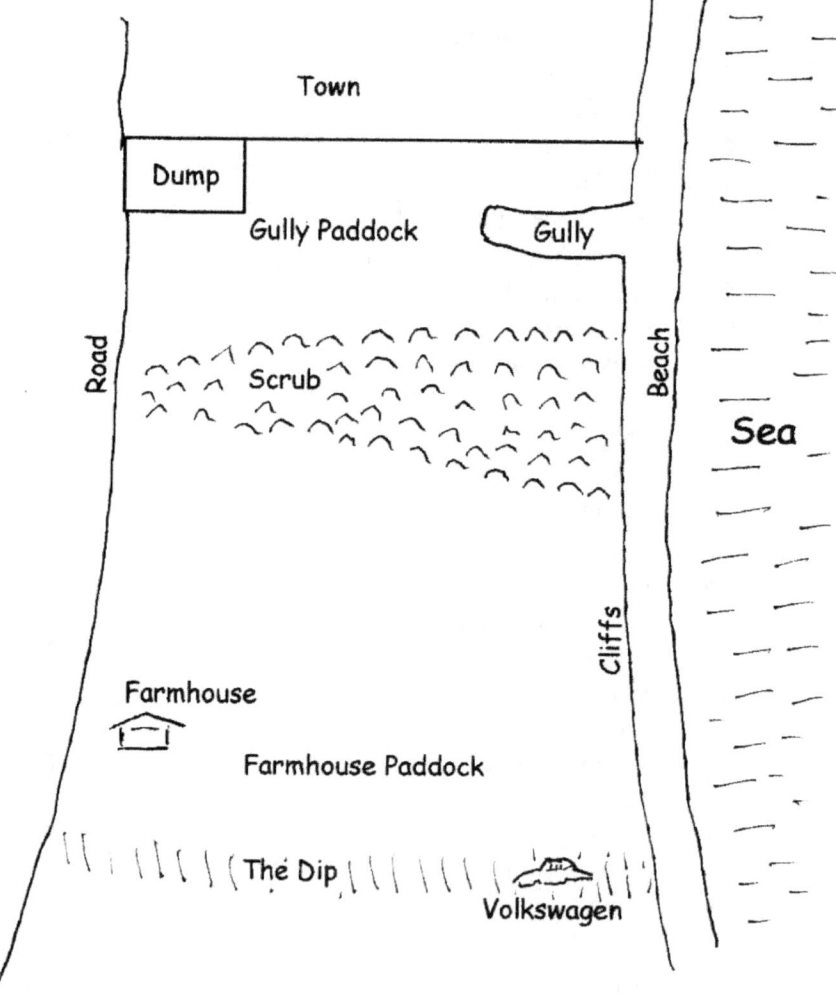

1

THE GREAT ESCAPE

Kuma peered through the bars of the prison and wondered what had happened to Jock. There had been three dogs in the pound up until a short while ago, but now he only had Milo for company. The dogcatcher had taken Jock away.

Kuma was a first timer, picked up on the streets for being unregistered, but Milo was a repeat offender. Milo knew the pound routine well, for he was always jumping the fence and going for walks. The dogcatcher had arrested him many times, the charge always the same, loitering without a lead. His owner was always bailing him out.

Kuma had been worried all day, for Milo and Jock had acted strangely that morning. They had been whispering in the corner, apparently plotting something. Kuma had asked Jock what it was they were talking about, but Jock would say nothing. This had hurt Kuma because Jock was his best friend.

'Do you think we will ever see Jock again?' Kuma asked.

Milo did not answer. He appeared to be listening to a noise coming from somewhere outside. However, the lack of answer did not surprise Kuma, for Milo was always ignoring him. Milo was top dog in the pound, and he considered Kuma to be a softie. Softies were never treated with respect.

Finally, Milo turned his attention to Kuma. 'What were you just saying?'

'I asked if Jock would be coming back.'

'No.'

The one word answer surprised Kuma. 'Where has he gone?'

Milo hesitated, but it was time for Kuma to know his fate. 'To the gas.'

'What?' exclaimed Kuma.

Milo looked away, and then he said. 'Jock has been here seven days. If no one claims you after seven days, you are declared homeless, and this place is death row for homeless dogs. How many days have you been here, Kuma?'

Kuma needed more information. *What does a row of death look like, and where is the gas?* he wondered.

'How many days?' Milo repeated.

However, Milo already knew that Kuma and Jock had been arrested together, and Kuma wondered why Milo would ask a question when he already knew the answer. Kuma and Jock had spent a wonderful time wandering the streets, chasing cats, and rummaging through garbage bins. The adventure would still be happening had the dogcatcher not cornered them in an alley. The dogcatcher had lassoed Jock with a catch pole and thrown him into the paddy wagon. Kuma had to act quickly or be separated from his friend, so he jumped into the paddy wagon with Jock. He could still remember Jock's words as the dogcatcher slammed the door.

'What are you doing in here you idiot? You're supposed to be running away, not taking a ride with me.'

Kuma had been upset by Jock's reprimand, for Jock had never called him an idiot before.

'How many days?' Milo asked for a third time.

'Seven, I suppose,' mumbled Kuma.

Silence followed, as Kuma thought about the unfairness of his situation. He was less than a year old, far too young to have fallen foul of the law. Born into a family of show dogs, his ears had been his downfall. One was shorter than the other, an unfortunate disfigurement for a show dog. His owner had tried to sell him, but in vain. A big, black, bullmastiff, with the strength of a lion and the appetite of a horse, was not an ideal family pet. Kuma had been dumped in the street and left to roam.

Suddenly, they heard the dogcatcher's footsteps. 'Well, this is it then,' said Milo. 'You and Jock have been here seven days. Jock has already done the walk of death. Now it's your turn.' Milo gave a strange laugh.

Kuma was startled by Milo's outburst, but at least it made one thing clear. Death row was a place where homeless dogs died, and Jock and he were homeless. However, Milo would be going home because Milo had a home to go to. He could not understand why Milo would laugh. Milo had to be the smuggest, most horrible, and most insensitive dog Kuma had ever known. For the first time in his life, he felt the urge to rip someone apart, but then the target of his anger stopped laughing. The dogcatcher was close, and they could hear him whistling.

'Do you know the name of that tune?' Milo asked.

Kuma did not know the answer, nor did he care. The whistling just added fuel to his anger. Milo had been laughing and the dogcatcher was whistling. Everyone seemed happy that Jock was gone and that he was about to die. Milo answered his own question. 'That song is called "Scotland the Brave". I think it's a nice gesture coming from a man who has just gassed a Scottish Terrier.'

That was the last straw. Kuma had to bite someone, but the dogcatcher was now his favoured target. However, he then remembered something his mum had told him. *A bullmastiff must never bite a human.* This meant that he could only bite Milo, but at least that would give Milo something to remember him by.

He glared at Milo as he planned his attack, but Kuma had never been in a dogfight before, nor had he ever bitten anyone before. He was still planning his attack when Milo pushed him into the corner and whispered in his ear. 'He hasn't seen you yet. Pretend you are asleep, and when I bark, you run.'

This sudden turn in events confused Kuma, for the laughing Milo was suddenly serious and telling him what to do. There was no time to think. Kuma had to rely on his instincts, and they were telling him to do as the older dog said. Kuma dropped in the corner and lay still, and the ruse worked. Moments later, the dogcatcher opened the door and assumed that Kuma was asleep. 'Wake up you lazy mutt,' he said.

Milo gave a sharp woof, and the dogcatcher looked away. Kuma sprang to his feet, but then he did something that Milo had not suggested. He knew he had to run, but the anger still boiled inside him. He had wanted to bite Milo, but Milo was now helping him escape. This left only the dogcatcher who was whistling "Scotland the Brave".

What Kuma did next, was something that he could never tell his mum. He sank his teeth hard into the dogcatcher's foot. There was a loud scream, so loud that Kuma barely heard Milo bark, 'Way to go, Kuma. You must forget your fears if you want to be free.'

Kuma headed for the pound gate, and there he found Jock waiting for him. 'I thought you were dead,' Kuma woofed, as he wagged his tail.

'Not me, laddie,' laughed Jock. 'That dogcatcher has a soft spot for us wee Scottish dogs, for he is a Scot himself. We are of common heritage, and bonds born in the highlands of Scotland can never be broken.'

'He just lets you go then?'

'He never tries to catch me, laddie. It was you he was after. He has no mercy for ugly dogs of British heritage.'

'I might be of British heritage, but I'm not ugly,' Kuma protested.

'You are far from cute,' chuckled Jock.

'You are just saying that because I have one ear shorter than the other.'

Jock tilted his head and looked at Kuma front on. 'I hadn't noticed that before, but now that you mention it, you are a bit lopsided.'

For a brief moment, Kuma wondered why it was that he liked Jock, but then they saw the dogcatcher hobbling toward them. The catch pole was still in his hand.

'We have to run,' Jock barked. 'I will show you a safe place to hide down at the wharfs.'

The two dogs hurried away, Jock pumping his little legs while Kuma loped behind. The dogcatcher stopped, for Kuma's bite had done him an injury. He turned and limped back to the pound.

Once safely away, Kuma needed to rest. 'You're a bit unfit for a young fella,' said Jock. 'I think you need to get rid of some of that fat.'

'Stop being rude to me,' said Kuma. 'That's my puppy fat, and it will go when it's ready.'

Jock changed the subject. 'Well at least you did a good job on the dogcatcher's foot, or he would still be chasing us.'

'What do you mean?' Kuma asked. He felt ashamed for having bitten a human, but fortunately, only Milo had witnessed the foul deed.

'I'm talking about the dogcatcher's injured foot,' said Jock.

Kuma shrugged. 'He must have caught it in something.'

Jock laughed. 'I think that something might have been your jaws, laddie.'

'I don't think so,' said Kuma. 'Biting a human is an unforgivable crime for a bullmastiff. Such an offence would tarnish my reputation forever. Why would you say such a thing?'

'His boot was in your mouth when you came running out.'

The damning evidence was stacked high. Kuma had to come clean. 'You say that I had his boot in my mouth?'

'Aye, laddie, his boot was in your mouth.'

Kuma sighed with relief. 'Thank goodness it was only his boot. I thought I had bitten his foot off.'

Jock chuckled. 'Good for you, killer. That dogcatcher had your measure, and someone had to get you angry or you would never have escaped. That's why Milo and I made a plan to get you mad, and Milo must have done a good job.'

2

A DOG ON THE RUN

The two dogs arrived at the wharfs and found a trawler berthed. Its crew was mending a net that they had spread along the dock, and the trawler smelt of fish.

'Come on, laddie, I need to introduce you to my friend, Jason. It looks like he'll be in port for a couple of days while they fix that net.'

Jason worked on the trawler, and he loved dogs. There had been a time when he had taken Jock to sea, but Jock preferred his paws to be on dry land.

'I've been to sea on that fine vessel,' said Jock.

'What's it like at sea?' asked Kuma.

Jock frowned. 'It's terrible, laddie. That boat pitches and rolls, everything gets wet, and I saw not a tree for a week; but you might like it.'

'Not me,' said Kuma,' 'That smell of fish is enough to put me off.'

Jason was sitting on an upturned bucket, mending a section of net that he had stretched across his knees. Jock bounded up and Jason patted him on the head. Then Jason noticed Kuma. 'Here fella,' he beckoned, but Kuma held back. Kuma thought that he might be in trouble if he trod on the net.

Jason beckoned again. 'Come on, don't be afraid; come here.'

Kuma advanced cautiously, his eyes fixed on Jason, closely watching for any hostile movement. Jason held out the back of his hand, inviting Kuma to give it a sniff. Jason loved dogs and this was his way of gaining their trust.

Kuma stretched forward and sniffed the hand, his legs tensed, ready to run should the hand do something unexpected. It passed inspection, and so Kuma took another step forward. Jason reached out and patted Kuma on the side, making sure that Kuma could see everything the hand was doing. Jason knew that to pat a strange dog in an unseen place would most likely cause the dog to run, or worse still, bite.

With the formal greetings over, Jason went back to mending the net with the two dogs stretched out beside him. Kuma was almost asleep when he felt the net being dragged beneath his tummy.

'Sorry to wake you, fella,' said Jason, 'but I need that net you are lying on.'

Kuma stirred but found it hard to move. He was at peace in the warm sun, and a kind voice had just said, 'sorry.' No one had ever spoken to him that way before. He was a dog people avoided. Kindness from a human was something Kuma had never known. The moment felt special.

'Shift yah big lump,' growled Jason. 'I can't fix this thing with you lying on it.' He pulled hard on the net and the special moment was broken. Kuma thought that he was in trouble. He ran to a distant spot on the wharf, as far from the net as he could get. Jason pulled the next section onto his knees. 'You can come back now,' he called.

Kuma did not move. 'You can come back,' yapped Jock, but Kuma still did not move. 'What's the problem?' Jock asked.

'He called me a big lump. He doesn't like me.'

'Don't be so over sensitive,' laughed Jock. 'Jason calls everyone names. He calls me a Scottish Bagpipe if I bark too much.'

At that moment, a voice came from the deck of the trawler. 'Hey Jason, you had better get those mutts hidden. The dogcatcher's van is heading this way.'

Jason looked up, but he did not have to move, for Jock had things under control. He bounded across the wharf and leapt onto the trawler's deck. 'Hurry Kuma, we have to hide,' he yapped.

Kuma followed, but then stopped when he saw how far he had to jump. He was not designed to do circus tricks. He looked down the gap that separated the trawler from the wharf and saw water. To fall down that crevice would have him swimming in the sea.

The dogcatcher's van pulled onto the wharf, and Jason could see Kuma's dilemma. He ran over and grabbed Kuma by the collar, and then leapt onto the trawler. Kuma was dragged through the air and they both landed on the deck. However, it would be more correct to say that Jason landed on the deck and Kuma landed on top of Jason. Kuma wondered how it was that Jason was suddenly sprawled beneath him, and he felt an urge to apologise. He licked Jason on the face.

'Get off you big lump, your breath stinks,' spluttered Jason. He pushed Kuma aside and staggered to his feet.

'Quick, get in here.' Jock yapped.

Jock was hiding in an open crate and Kuma jumped in beside him. They both watched the dogcatcher get out of his van. He was carrying a fishing rod.

'Are you going to do some fishing, mate?' yelled Jason, who now had dog slobber all over his face.

'Yep. I injured my foot at work and got the rest of the day off.'

'How did you do that?' Jason asked.

The dogcatcher ran a wary eye along the wharf. 'I was attacked by a savage dog. He's a big, black, ugly brute that people need to avoid because the mongrel bites.'

'He sounds like one of those dogs that slobber everywhere,' said Jason, as he wiped away the slobber from his face.

'He does that alright,' said the dogcatcher. 'Have you seen him?'

'No,' said Jason, as he checked that all the slobber was gone.

Kuma was puzzled. 'I haven't seen an ugly, black brute of a dog around here, have you?' he asked Jock.

'I think he means you, laddie,' Jock chuckled.

'That couldn't be me,' exclaimed Kuma. 'He's looking for a mongrel. I come from a long line of show dogs.'

Jock laughed. 'Tell that to the dogcatcher.'

Kuma thought back to his family, and those happy days of growing up with his brother, Ulysses, and his sister, Portia. No one ever called them ugly, even though they looked no different to him. He remembered them being sold to nice people and his mum saying that he would be going to a loving home too, but she was wrong. He was just taken away and dumped without being given a chance to say goodbye to her.

The dogcatcher limped to the edge of the wharf, close to the bow of the trawler. There he settled for an afternoon's fishing, not knowing that Kuma and Jock were hiding nearby. Suddenly, he shouted, 'Got one.'

'Got a fish, mate?' called Jason.

'Yep, a beauty. I reckon I will fish here for the rest of the day.'

Jock looked at Kuma and shook his head.

'What's wrong?' Kuma whispered.

'I think you are the unluckiest dog I've ever met,' smiled Jock.

Kuma frowned. 'What makes you say that?'

Jock glared in the direction of the dogcatcher. 'I can roam the streets on my own, and he never comes near me, but when I team up with you, he puts me in the pound.'

'So,' said Kuma.

Jock continued to glare. 'So I bring you to my favourite hiding place, and he turns up. He has never been here before, but today he comes and stays.'

'How is this my fault?' snorted Kuma, not wanting to be blamed for the dogcatcher's bad behaviour.

Jock shrugged. 'Kuma, you are a trouble magnet.'

Kuma had never heard of a trouble magnet, but he said no more. Jock had won the argument.

3

ALL AT SEA

The two dogs remained cramped in the crate and waited for the dogcatcher to leave, but he stayed. Nothing changed until late that afternoon. By then, the net had been mended and was back on the trawler, which meant the crew was ready to put to sea.

'We are about to leave,' Jason yelled to the dogcatcher. 'You will have to move until we are gone.'

'I will wait by the van,' came the reply.

Kuma glared at Jock. 'I thought you said that the trawler would be in port for a couple of days.'

Jock shrugged. 'I guess I was wrong.'

'What shall we do?' asked Kuma.

The trawler's motor roared to life. 'Cast off,' shouted the skipper.

'We have to make a run for it,' yapped Jock. He jumped out of the crate and ran to the trawler's side-rail. From there, he sprung onto the wharf. 'Follow me,' he barked.

Kuma ran to the side-rail but was afraid to jump. The dogcatcher saw him from his van. Moments later, Kuma and the dogcatcher were face to face, barely an arm's length apart, but the dogcatcher could do nothing. The gap between trawler and wharf was widening. His quarry was so close but getting away. Meanwhile, Jock had bounded to the end of the wharf, but the dogcatcher was not interested in catching him. Instead, he glared at Kuma. 'You will be back, and I will be waiting,' he growled.

Kuma had narrowly escaped one problem, but he still had another. His only friend was back on the wharf, and like with his mum, they had been torn apart without a proper farewell. He felt frightened, trapped on a boat that was going to pitch and roll, a boat that was going to be wet, and a boat that smelt of fish. This experience he would be sharing with humans he knew nothing about. He looked back at a diminishing black dot on the wharf. This would probably be the last time that he would ever see Jock.

The trawler was soon in open water, and Kuma felt it begin to pitch. He peered back to the wharf, but the black dot was gone. Strangely, none of the crew had noticed his accidental inclusion on the passenger list, but that soon changed. The skipper looked down from the wheelhouse. 'Jason, we have a stowaway. Have you brought one of your mutts on board?'

Jason ran to the stern and found Kuma. 'He's a friend of Jock's, Skipper, but I guess he's my responsibility now.'

'Well, let's hope that he makes a better sailor than Jock,' laughed the skipper.

Jason looked at Kuma's collar, which proudly bore its wearer's name. 'His name is Kuma.'

The skipper shook his head. 'Best show Kuma around the ship and then give him a feed. He might have a rough trip ahead of him.'

'Aye aye, Skipper.'

Jason took Kuma for a stroll around the deck, and Kuma was surprised to find everything dry. Jock had said that everything would be wet, but not so. Jock told him that the boat pitched and rolled, but Kuma liked the feeling. He looked over the side-rail and saw foam coming from the bow. It rushed past in an endless stream, laying a white trail to mark their journey. He filled his lungs with sea air and relished its freshness. The air had a tang that complemented the fishy odour of the boat. But the best was yet to come.

'Ready for something to eat, big fella?' said Jason. 'We eat nothing but the finest food on this vessel.'

The cook had handed Jason a bowl of stew and its delicious aroma was like nothing Kuma had ever known. His mouth watered, for he had not eaten all day. He thought it strange that Jock had not mentioned that there was excellent food on the boat. Jock had made everything sound bad.

Kuma followed his meal to a sheltered spot behind the wheelhouse. To his surprise, he discovered that Jason had set up a dog bed and water bowl there. 'We bought all this for Jock, but he didn't go much for it,' said Jason. 'You can stay here during the day and sleep in my cabin at night.'

The other crewmembers gathered to watched Kuma eat, and the bowl was soon licked clean. 'I guess he wants more,' one crewmember said. 'Hey, cookie, our mascot wants more stew.' The cook brought another bowl from the galley.

Kuma was in heaven. He began eating his second serve, but it was more food than he had ever eaten before. He slowed his chewing and then stopped. This drew some unusual comments from the crew.

'I bet he can't finish,' said one.

'I bet he can,' said another.

'You're on,' said the first. 'Does anyone else want to take my bet?'

'I will,' came a shout from behind.

Everyone gathered close, and Kuma wondered what was going on. Some began to chant, 'Eat, Kuma, eat.'

The situation caused Kuma to remember something his mum had once told him. *Some humans are kind, but some are cruel. Some you can trust, but some you can't. No two humans are alike, but they all think that they are smarter than dogs, which makes them unpredictable.*

Jason picked up the bowl. 'All bets are off, fellas. Kuma is carrying a bit of flab. He needs to be put on a diet.'

It's only puppy fat, thought Kuma. He was sick of people saying that he was overweight. People had once said that he was cute, but that was when he was little. Now, everyone said that he needed to diet, but fortunately, Jason's idea of a diet was to be served big helpings of scrumptious stew. Kuma could handle that diet. *I wonder what Jock and Milo had for dinner tonight,* he thought.

With eating over, Kuma retired to his dog bed. From there, he watched the changing vista of the sunset. He saw the sky turn pink, then red, and then the sun disappeared below the sea. Darkness fell, but then a bright light came on from the masthead. It lit up the boat's deck as if it were day. Kuma rested, his senses lulled by the soothing motion of the waves. He felt content.

Sometime later, Jason appeared from the wheelhouse. He had been rostered for the early morning watch, which meant that he needed an early night. He patted Kuma on the head. 'Come on, fella, it's time for shut-eye. You have another bunk waiting downstairs.'

Jason opened the door behind the wheelhouse and led Kuma down steps that led to the engine room. They walked past the throbbing motor and then through another door that opened into Jason's cabin. The cabin was small and held little besides a double bunk. 'I guess you want the bottom bunk,' said Jason.

Kuma hopped onto the bunk, and Jason climbed the ladder to the one above, but then Kuma hopped back onto the floor.

Jason looked down. 'Go to sleep, Kuma. I've given you my bottom bunk. What more do you want?'

Jason turned out the light, not knowing that he was about to expose Kuma's greatest fear. Kuma was afraid of the dark. For a short while, there was silence, but then Jason heard a small, but pitiful whine. He put his head under the blankets, but the whining grew louder. Jason turned on the light and discovered Kuma still sitting on the floor.

'What do you want?' Jason sighed.

Kuma stood on his hind legs and pawed the side of Jason's bunk.

'You can't get up here,' growled Jason. 'You don't know how to climb a ladder.'

Kuma continued clawing the bunk, dragging Jason's blankets to the floor.

'That's it,' said Jason. 'I'm having the bottom bunk and you can sleep where you are.' He grabbed his pillow and settled on the bottom bunk, but things did not stay that way for long. Jason felt the bunk sag as Kuma joined him. 'Okay, you can sleep here if you like, but get down the far end and don't complain if I kick you in the head.'

That was the invitation Kuma wanted, and he was not concerned about kicks to the head. The dark harboured scary monsters that Kuma could not see, and the safety of sleeping on Jason's bed was well worth the risk of a kick.

At 2.00 a.m., the skipper appeared at the door. 'Time for your watch, Jason.'

Half asleep, Jason tried to stumble out of bed, but he found an unfamiliar lump in his bunk. He poked the lump, but it did not move. He began to climb over the lump, but that was when the lump woke up. Kuma lifted his head, Jason lost his balance, and next, Jason was lying flat on the floor. Kuma could not resist. A big, sloppy tongue washed Jason's face. Fortunately, there was no slobber this time, but Jason still complained. 'Phew, your breath stinks. Next time, shift when I get out of bed.'

Kuma ignored Jason's complaint. He wagged his tail, for Jason had said, 'next time.' That meant that he would get to sleep on Jason's bunk again. He wondered about his bad breath, however. As owner of the breath, he was closest to it, and he had never once detected an odour. He concluded that Jason was one of those grumpy, morning people.

Kuma followed Jason to the wheelhouse, for Kuma was afraid to be left in the cabin alone. He watched Jason take the wheel and assume command of the vessel. The wheelhouse was an exciting place that had a steering wheel, two odd looking televisions with blue screens, a third television with a round screen, and a box with knobs and dials. Kuma looked at the televisions but saw nothing of interest. However, they filled the room with a soft, blue glow, and Jason had no need to switch on the light.

The sea was calm, but as the night went on, the wind picked up and the waves became higher. Undaunted, the trawler ploughed on. At times, its bow would rise high above a wave and then drop into the valley beyond. At other times, a wave would almost bring the boat to a halt. The air was filled with spray, and Kuma could see why Jock had said everything was always wet. Jock had said that he hated life at sea, but Kuma found it exciting.

Once Jason's shift was over, Kuma ran to the bow where he could best feel the wind in his face. He felt the waves lift him high, and he would look down upon them. Next, the bow would fall, and a wave would be charging him head on. In defiance, the bow of the trawler would then slice the wave in half, casting its remnants aside in sheets of spray. Kuma barked as each decisive blow was struck.

Kuma rode his trusty trawler as it slew the oncoming foe. He led the charge until victory was in sight. The waves became smaller, and then they surrendered. The sea ahead was calm, and beyond that was land. The trawler was headed toward a small town sprawled along the top of a cliff. Below the cliff was a narrow beach.

As they got closer, Kuma could see people, and then seagulls came out to greet them. The engines slowed and the trawler edged its way into a short jetty. There were a number of fishermen on the jetty, and several had to move to make way for the trawler. Ropes were thrown and made fast, and then the engines fell silent.

'I'm going ashore to do some trading,' said the skipper. 'You can all go ashore but be back well before end of tide. If we stay too long, we will lose the water in the channel.'

The skipper often called at the town on his voyages. He would visit his farmer friend and exchange fish for farm produce. These visits were the reason for the boat's excellent cuisine.

4

THE CASTAWAY

Jason hopped over the boat's side-rail and onto the jetty. 'Come on, Kuma, we're going for a walk.'

Kuma sized up the jump, but it was too hard. Jock had made it look easy, but Kuma was not a jumping dog. He stayed put, causing Jason to hop back on the trawler. Jason stacked some fish boxes to make stairs for Kuma to climb. 'Climb up here, Kuma, and jump onto the jetty,' he said.

Kuma understood and climbed to the top of the boxes. Jason was impressed by how quickly Kuma had understood the command. 'You're a very smart dog,' he complimented.

Kuma wagged his tail, for he was not used to compliments.

'Now jump.'

Jason was no longer impressed, for Kuma just looked at him. Climbing stairs had been one thing, but jumping through thin air required a different set of skills. Jason sighed. He hopped onto the jetty and grabbed Kuma by the collar. 'Is this how I have to get you over the side-rail every time?' he growled. He pulled on Kuma's collar and the same thing happened as before. Jason finished flat on his back with Kuma on top of him.

Kuma could hear laughter coming from the old blokes who were fishing on the jetty, and he wondered what they were laughing at. Something funny had just happened, but he had missed it because Jason had pulled his collar at the wrong time. It appeared that Jason had also missed the joke, because Jason was the only human not laughing. He was holding his hands to his face anticipating another lick. *Why would he not want me to lick his face?* thought Kuma. Jason picked himself up and brushed off his clothes. The laughter continued, but Jason ignored it. 'Come on, Kuma, let's check out the town.'

Kuma followed Jason into the main street of what appeared to be a friendly, little town, but Kuma began to worry. People were staring at him in a strange way. They came across a man who was putting up posters.

'What's all this about,' Jason asked.

The man looked at Jason and then glared at Kuma. 'I take it that you were not at the town meeting last night.'

'No.'

'Well, if you had been there, you would know that your dog should be on a leash.' He pointed to the poster.

ALL STRAY DOGS WILL BE SHOT ON SIGHT

Jock was right when he had called Kuma the unluckiest dog he had ever met. With perfect timing, Kuma had arrived in the town the morning following the town's crisis meeting. A pack of dogs had been roaming the district and harassing sheep. The meeting had labelled them the "Sheep Killers" and deemed that all stray dogs were now outlaws and were to be shot.

'I suggest you keep your dog close,' said the man. 'There are a lot of trigger-happy farmers around here, and that dog of yours could find himself full of bullets.' Kuma had no idea what a bullet was, but he hoped that it was something nice to eat.

Jason looked about and could see the hostility of the townsfolk. The safest place for Kuma was on the beach. Farmers would have no cause to shoot a dog on a beach, because a beach was not a place where they grazed sheep. He went back to the jetty and then down onto the sand. Kuma followed.

The beach was a new experience for Kuma, for he could see many things of interest, and all needed his attention. First was a dead sea bird. It had an irresistible aroma, and so Kuma pushed it with his snout. 'Get away from that rotten thing,' yelled Jason.

I was only looking, thought Kuma, as he moved on to find more treasures. It was then that he saw a dog in the water. The dog was black and had a head the same size as his, but the head was all that Kuma could see.

Kuma stared at the head but could see no ears. He had been rejected because he had one ear shorter than the other. A dog with no ears would be an outcast for sure. It was no wonder that the dog was out in the water. Nasty people had probably chased it there.

Kuma shouted a friendly woof and bounded out to join the dog. At knee deep, he discovered that the water was cold, and so he bounded back to the beach. The head disappeared and then surfaced further along. Kuma chased after it, barking as he went.

'Come here, Kuma, and stop chasing that stupid seal,' Jason shouted, but Kuma was too excited to take notice. He was chasing a dog just like himself, only this dog was a much better swimmer.

'Hey, Mr Dog, come back, I want to talk to you,' Kuma woofed, but the unsociable dog just kept on swimming. Finally, Kuma gave up. He could run no further. He had things in common with that dog and they could have been good friends, but the other dog was being a snob.

Kuma lay on a cool patch of seaweed with no intention of moving, but his rest ended when Jason caught up with him. They had to get back to the trawler before it sailed, and Kuma had taken them much further than Jason had intended. 'Bad dog,' he said. 'Now we have to hurry back to the boat,' but Kuma could see no reason to be called bad. The other dog was the one who had been rude.

They headed back to the jetty, but Kuma found the going hard because he was exhausted after chasing the unsociable dog. They got back just as the boat's engine started. The Skipper leaned out the wheelhouse. 'Hurry up, Jason. The tide won't wait for us.'

Jason ran to the trawler and jumped over the side-rail. He was hoping that Kuma was right behind, but Kuma was well back. He was walking slowly, his tongue hanging out as slobber drooled from his mouth. 'Come on, Kuma,' shouted Jason, but all was in vain. Water began to swirl around the trawler's stern and then the boat began to move. Even if Kuma had made the distance, there was no way that he could have jumped on board. In desperation, Jason pleaded to the fishermen on the jetty. 'Can one of you fellas look after my dog until I get back.'

Several gave a slight wave and a couple nodded.

Kuma watched the trawler as it headed out to sea with Jason looking back over the stern. Kuma had found a new home on that boat, but his luck had deserted him again. His life of riding the waves and eating gourmet food had ended in a day. His only hope was to stay close to the jetty and wait for the boat's return, not knowing when that might be. He went over and stood by the fishermen.

'Who is going to take the dog home?' shouted a fisherman, but the rest just kept on fishing. No one was prepared to look after Kuma. He was alone again and unaware of the hostility that awaited him in town. However, he had something more immediate to attend to. His adventure had made him thirsty.

5

THE HUNTED

Kuma walked back to a fish-cleaning table at the beginning of the jetty, for he had seen a puddle of water there, courtesy of a dripping tap. Drinking from puddles and raiding bins was how he had survived during his time with Jock. Jock had taught him everything a homeless dog needed to know, including the appreciation of garbage day.

Garbage day was the day when humans put out bins in which were presents for dogs. A present could be half a pizza, a burned pie, or perhaps a bone to chew. You never knew what surprise waited for you in a garbage bin, and there was a garbage bin next to the fish cleaning table, but Kuma's first priority was to drink.

Kuma sunk his tongue into the murky puddle, but unfortunately, his eagerness caused him to slurp too deep. He shook his head, snorted, and spat out mud. This caused a group of seagulls to laugh. Kuma glared at them but ignored their rudeness. Laughter seemed to be following him from one end of the jetty to the other.

Kuma continued to drink but with caution, and when he had finished, he decided to check the rubbish bin for treats. All he had to do was to push it over, and Kuma had never met a rubbish bin that he could not topple. His partnership with Jock had been the envy of the homeless dog community. Little Jock could only raid small bins before meeting Kuma, but after that, he could point to the largest of bins and simply say, 'Push that one over for me please, laddie.'

Kuma pushed the bin and its contents spewed onto the ground. There were fish heads, fish backbones, and fish guts, a true treasure-trove of dog delights. Kuma had never had so many presents from which to choose, and he wondered which to try first, but the rude gulls saw things differently. They came from everywhere and lay claim to Kuma's presents. Kuma woofed, but woofing proved useless. The gulls were experienced scavengers, and he was just a beginner. They were more interested in fighting each other and could not be bothered about him. He was simply a hindrance.

Kuma positioned his body over the booty and held his ground. He had noticed that the gulls were choosing to rush the fish guts first, so he thought he had better try them before they all went. However, the battle for fish guts proved so intense that Kuma retreated. *Perhaps I should try a backbone*, he thought. He reached to grab one, but a gull flapped in his face. He barked at the gull, but when he reached again, the backbone was gone. Another gull had stolen it. Kuma realised that the only way to beat the gulls was to eat quickly.

Kuma grabbed another backbone and began to chew. He found it prickly, but it tasted nice, and the harder bits were crunchie. He finished it and looked for another, but they were all gone. The greedy gulls had taken the lot. Some flew about with backbones in their beaks, avoiding others who were trying to snatch them away.

All that remained were the fish heads that were too heavy for the gulls to carry. They were pecking at them where they lay on the ground. Kuma chose a head and pushed the gulls aside. It tasted better than expected. He ate it and then crunched another, then another, and then another. Finally, he had eaten all the heads, much to the annoyance of the gulls.

Kuma left the jetty and wandered back to the main street where he had been that morning. He recalled the unfriendly stares of the people but hoped things would be better this time. Kuma was always the optimist, but this sometimes got him into trouble.

At first, the street seemed peaceful. Kuma watched the people as they strolled about, stopping at times to look in shop windows or talk to each other. Most of the vehicles were parked at the kerb with just a few moving along the street, but their slowness posed no danger to a dog. However, there were now more posters than before and all carried the same message, but Kuma could not read. Suddenly, there came the shout that turned the peaceful street into Kuma's worst nightmare.

'Stray dog!' People came from everywhere.

'Does anybody own him?' came a shout.

'That brute doesn't belong in sheep country,' came another.

'Call the police,' came a third.

Kuma saw the same hostile glares that people had given him that morning, and his heart began to race. But then came a voice from someone he thought was a friend. An old man who spent his days sitting outside the hardware store, had been one of the few to have smiled at him that morning. He had even patted Kuma on the head.

'I know him,' said the old man. He came past this morning, following that lad from the trawler. I reckon he's a stray.'

The treacherous old bloke had sealed Kuma's fate.

'Someone call the cop,' shouted MacLeod, who owned the farm just south of the town. 'The rest of you surround him. We can hold him here until the law arrives.' MacLeod saw it as his duty to take charge.

Kuma should have run, but he had left his run too late. MacLeod was holding a shovel, and he was within easy striking distance of Kuma's head. Kuma cowered to the ground as a crowd gathered. A hostile cordon soon had him surrounded. The old man went into the hardware store and brought out axe handles. Everyone was given a weapon.

Kuma stayed crouched in the middle of the road, surrounded by the mob. He sensed that most would wish him no harm, but his mum had warned him that humans were unpredictable. He thought that the crew on the trawler had acted strangely when they surrounded him while he was eating, but these people were doing the same thing, only they were doing it with malice.

MacLeod became impatient. 'We can't block the road forever,' he said. 'You lot keep an eye on him while I get my gun.' He walked to his truck, taking the shovel with him. Kuma felt relieved to see the shovel go, but he had never heard of a gun.

MacLeod returned with a rifle, which caused some in the crowd to gasp. Kuma looked at the weapon but saw no threat. The only thing he feared was the loop at the end of a catch pole.

'I'm not sure that you are allowed to shoot a gun in town,' came a voice from the crowd.

'You're not even supposed to have a gun in town,' said a woman who was standing back from the rest.

'These are extreme times, and they require extreme measures,' said MacLeod. He walked toward Kuma and pulled back the rifle's bolt. A bullet slipped into the breach. He paused, and then pushed the bolt forward. The gun was cocked and ready to fire. He aimed the weapon at Kuma's head.

Kuma listened to the strange clicks and clunks made by the rifle. They fascinated him, and he wondered if the rifle was a plaything. Perhaps MacLeod wanted a game. He sat up, put his head to one side, and looked at MacLeod. His tail twitched an expectant wag. Some in the crowd turned their backs.

MacLeod hesitated and stepped back. 'I can't do it,' he said. 'I've never shot a dog, and I don't think I can. The police will have to deal with him.'

The old man called out, 'You have to do it. It's your duty to the district.'

MacLeod shook his head and walked away.

With MacLeod gone, the old man took charge. 'We are making a citizen's arrest,' he said. 'This dog goes nowhere until the police arrive.'

The police van soon appeared. 'Where's the stray?' yelled the young constable as he stepped from the vehicle. Kuma ignored him at first, but then he noticed that the constable had a catch pole. The crowd with their axe handles had been intimidating, but a man with a catch pole was far more dangerous. A catch pole was the thing humans used to seek a dog's destruction. Kuma froze, but then he remembered Milo's words. 'You must forget your fears if you want to be free.'

Kuma looked at the crowd, for someone had to suffer if he were to escape. The women would be easy to push and the youngsters even easier, but the person to pay the price for his freedom should be someone who deserved it.

The treacherous old man shouted, 'Kill him,' and that was his big mistake. Kuma was not a leaping dog, but that old man was worth the

23

effort. Kuma flew through the air and flattened the turncoat to the ground, and then he pushed his snout into the old man's face. There were no more shouts of, 'Kill him,' for Kuma's victim dared not to open his mouth. His beard was full of dog slobber.

Kuma ran to the beach with the young constable close behind. The water offered sanctuary, and Kuma could see why the unsociable dog had learned to swim so well. However, Kuma was not a good swimmer. He began running to where he last saw the unsociable dog. A short time later, he looked back. The young constable had given up the chase.

6

A MONSTER IN THE DARK

Kuma walked along the beach, hoping to find the unsociable dog, but his fellow outcast was nowhere to be seen. He kept on walking and then detected a strange odour in the air. It was like nothing he had ever known, for it was many smells rolled into one. The smell demanded his attention, but it would have to wait.

The narrow beach lay between tall cliffs and a smooth sea. Kuma had surveyed the coast from the trawler and concluded that the cliffs were far too steep for a dog to climb. However, he had noticed a gully some distance from the jetty, which he thought would be a place where he could leave the beach. He suspected that the unsociable dog would have gone that way himself.

Kuma came to the gully and walked along its dry watercourse. The gully walls were steep, and beneath them grew an abundance of bushes. However, the gully ended after only a short distance before coming to some steps cut by humans. Kuma ran up the steps and found himself on open ground, but nowhere could he see the unsociable dog. However, a flock of seagulls was gathered nearby, and the strange odour had become much stronger.

The seagulls had gathered in an area that was surrounded by a wire fence, and the odour seemed to be coming from there. To Kuma, the place looked like a theme park built for dogs. The gate was open, and he wondered if that was where the unsociable dog lived.

Kuma ran through the gate and found himself in a wonderland of old cars, dumped fridges, and rusty water tanks. The seagulls were feasting on a pile of fish offal. Kuma wandered over to join them.

'Who told you about this place?' asked a gull.

'No one,' said Kuma. 'I don't even know what this place is.'

'It's the local dump and you aren't welcome,' came the reply. 'You have already stolen fish from us today.'

'They were my fish,' growled Kuma. 'I was the one who pushed the bin over. If they were your fish, the humans wouldn't have put them in the bin in the first place.'

'That's a good point,' said a gull, 'but humans do strange things. We tell them to throw the fish on the beach near town, but they ignore us. They choose to put the fish in bins, bring the bins out here, and then throw the fish on the ground. It's a waste of effort on their part, and it forces us to come all the way out here to eat.'

At that moment, a truck arrived, and a bin of fish offal was tipped onto the ground. The seagulls hovered over the men from the truck. 'Why don't you just tip it on the beach by the jetty,' they screeched, but the men did not understand. However, one of them saw Kuma.

'Isn't that the stray they tried to catch in town today?' he said to his friend.

'Looks like it,' said the other. 'Best we shut the gate and lock him in for the night. The law can deal with him in the morning.'

'Better run, dog, or you'll be locked in,' warned the gulls. Kuma wanted to run, but he was afraid to run past the men. He watched them shut the gate and drive away. 'Too late now,' the gulls laughed.

Kuma ignored the taunts. He was an optimist. He would find another way out, but first he wanted to eat, and the gulls had already devoured half the delivery. He joined them.

'Beat it, dog,' squawked the gulls.

'No, let him eat,' came one lone squawk.

'Why?' squawked the rest.

The lone gull spoke. 'They will be coming for him in the morning, and he can't get away. We should let him enjoy his last meal in peace.'

The feeding frenzy stopped, and the gulls looked at Kuma. He thought that they were feeling sympathy for his plight. 'Is there another way out?' he asked, but their apparent sympathy was short lived. A gull grabbed the backbone Kuma was eating and the rest went back to their food fight. Kuma was finding it hard to like seagulls.

Fortunately, there was enough fish for everyone. Once Kuma had finished, he washed down his meal with a drink from an upturned hubcap. He then walked the perimeter fence looking for a hole, but there were none to be found. The seagulls were right. He was trapped, and the man with the catch pole would be coming for him in the morning. However, there was one thing that he feared more than a man with a catch pole, and that was being alone in the dark—and it was getting dark.

Kuma found an upturned boat and crawled under it. To his surprise, there was some old bedding there. He curled up and made himself comfortable, and then his thoughts turned to the unsociable dog. Trying to befriend him had been a mistake. He could have spent the day riding the waves, eating stew, and he would now be sleeping on the end of Jason's bed. Instead, he was in a rubbish dump, eating fish offal, and darkness was closing in around him.

Kuma lay with his eyes wide open. He sniffed the air for the scent of creatures unknown, but the smell of the dump was overwhelming. Darkness fell, and inside the boat was total blackness. He strained his ears, listening for things that he could not see, and then he peered outside. There he saw dark shapes silhouetted against a star filled sky. He glared at the shapes, watching for signs of movement. Suddenly, something crawled on his leg. He yelped and hit his head on the boat's upturned hull.

'Sorry about that,' came a voice from nowhere.

'D- did someone j-just say s-sorry,' stammered Kuma.

'Only me,' came a perky reply.

'Who are you?'

'Just a mouse. We are all around you.'

'Hi, Mr Dog,' chorused a gathering of mice.

Kuma was not alone after all. He had mice for company. 'What are you all doing here?' he asked.

'We're playing dare devils,' came the reply. 'It's our scary game. If she catches you, you are dead. Not straight away, mind you. She likes to torture her victims first.'

'Who is she?' trembled Kuma.

The mouse put on his scariest voice. 'She is huge, has sharp teeth, and even sharper claws. She hears the slightest noise and can see in the dark. She is silent and sneaks up on her victims without them knowing.'

'Aren't you all scared?' Kuma asked.

'It's a numbers game,' laughed the mouse. 'There are lots of us and only one of her. Each of us thinks that she will catch someone else. Besides, it's easy for us to run and hide.'

Kuma was not sure that he understood mouse logic, but they had given him good reason to be afraid of the dark. There was a real monster out there. The mice could hide, but he was too big. He tried to crawl under his bedding. 'Where does she live?' he mumbled.

'Here, in the dump,' the mouse explained. 'Actually, you're sleeping on her bed.'

No sooner were these words said before a small voice squeaked, 'Run, she's coming.'

Kuma sensed the sudden scurry around him. 'Are you all still there?' he asked, but there was only silence. Kuma was alone.

7

FACING YOUR WORST FEARS

Kuma tried again to put his head under the bedding but only managed to cover his snout. He closed his eyes, but then realised that safety required them open. Either way, the dark was still the same. He tried holding back his whimpers so that he could listen, but it was all too hard. The monster could see in the dark, had sharp teeth, and could sneak up without him knowing.

'Go away, monster, go away,' Kuma whined, and then came a polite cough from outside the boat.

'Excuse me, but what are you carrying on about?'

'There's a monster out there,' Kuma whimpered, and then he wondered whom he was talking to.

'Really? I don't see a monster,' said the voice outside.

'W-who are you?' stammered Kuma.

'I'm not telling you until you tell me who you are.'

'Why.'

'Because you are sleeping in my bed.'

Horror upon horrors, he was talking to the monster. It had to be a bad dream. He sat up and banged his head once more. The whack felt real. This was not a dream.

'I'm sorry to be in your bed, but I'm afraid of monsters,' Kuma whimpered.

'But I can't see any monsters,' said the voice, 'but I can sure hear strange noises coming from under that boat. Come out here. I want to see what you look like.'

There are moments in life when people discover things they never knew about themselves, and this was one of those moments for Kuma. The monster in the dark that he had always feared, was suddenly real. However, the real monster seemed less frightening than the one he had always imagined. He poked his head out and saw a tall shape. It moved. Kuma showed his teeth and snarled.

'You're growling at a tree,' laughed the voice. 'I'm over here.'

Kuma looked toward the direction of the voice and saw another shape, but this shape was much smaller, about half-Jock-size, and Jock was a smallish dog. The shape came closer, for it wanted to examine the head poking out from under the boat.

'Are you a dog?' asked the shape.

'Of course, I'm a dog,' said Kuma.

'You have a very big head for a dog.'

'I'm a very big dog.'

'Then what are you afraid of. If you are a big dog, nothing should frighten you.'

'I'm afraid of the dark,' confessed Kuma.

'Oh, you have a problem then, because it gets dark every day around here.'

'It gets dark every day, everywhere,' said Kuma, 'but I guess nothing frightens you.'

'Only one thing.'

'And what's that?'

'Dogs.'

Kuma's monster in the dark was afraid of dogs, and he was a dog. That was an unexpected turn of events. 'You don't have to be frightened of me,' he said, 'I don't want to harm anyone.'

'Not even a cat?'

'I don't know any cats,' said Kuma. 'They all run away when they see me coming.'

'I am a cat,' said the shape.

'The mice said you were a monster.'

'Sometimes mice exaggerate.'

Kuma could feel his heart rate slow. The mice had indeed exaggerated. Kuma's mum had told him that cats were the sworn enemy of ordinary dogs, but bullmastiffs were above that sort of thing.

It was true that he had helped Jock to chase cats, but it had never been his idea.

'Why aren't you running away from me?' Kuma asked.

'Can you see where you are going in the dark?' asked the cat.

'No.'

'Then I won't bother to run, but I would like my bed back.'

'Can I stay too?' asked Kuma. 'I'm afraid of the dark.'

The cat thought a moment. 'Will you promise not to bite me?'

'I promise.'

'One false move, and I can scratch your eyes out.'

'Stop trying to scare me,' said Kuma. 'I've already promised that I won't bite.'

An agreement was made, and the two unlikely companions settled under the boat and exchanged their stories.

The cat was called Kitty, for she had never grown to the size of most cats. She was ginger, with a white tummy, and had recently moved into the dump because of problems at home. She was an excellent hunter but had enemies that she feared and was looking for an ally to protect her.

Kuma told his story, but he had no skills about which he could boast. He was just a simple dog on the run who was looking for a friend.

The two had things in common, and Kuma felt that they could be friends. He slept well that night and woke refreshed the next morning, but then he remembered the gate. A man would be coming with a catch pole. He ran to the gate and found it still locked.

'What's your problem now?' asked Kitty.

'The gate is locked.'

'So?'

'So I can't get out,' Kuma mumbled.

'Have you looked for a hole in the fence?'

'Of course, and there aren't any.'

'You had a boy look, didn't you?'

'What is a boy look?'

Kitty laughed. 'Boys never look properly, and when they do, they see things that aren't there.'

'I never see things that aren't there,' protested Kuma.

'Then why were you growling at a tree last night?'

Kuma had no answer.

'Come on,' said Kitty, 'let me show you the hole that you never saw. It is so big that even you can get through it.'

Kuma followed Kitty to some long grass at the back of the dump. 'I'm not going in there,' he said.

'Why?'

'Snakes.' Kuma did not know what a snake was, but his mum had told him that he should never go into long grass because a snake might get him.

'Don't worry about snakes,' said Kitty, 'they're all in bed.'

They pushed through the grass, and sure enough, the fence had a hole in it. 'You didn't look here did you?' Kitty asked.

'The hole is hidden by grass.'

'As I said, you had a boy look. Now stay with me, and I will give you a tour of my territory.'

8

MACLEOD'S FARM

Kitty's territory was MacLeod's farm, which was on a strip of land running along the coast. Cliffs bordered the farm on one side, as did a road on the other.

The farm had two large paddocks separated by a thick patch of scrub. The scrub ran from the road to the cliff top, dividing the farm in two.

The first paddock was called the gully paddock because the gully ran into it. The dump was in the corner of this paddock. The second paddock was called the farmhouse paddock, because that was where MacLeod had his farmhouse. This paddock was furthest from town.

'Would you like to see your old home,' said Kuma.

'We have to go through that scrub to get to the farmhouse,' said Kitty, 'and the scrub is a dangerous place.'

They were walking in the gully paddock, following a fence that ran close to the road, and the scrub was just ahead. 'Surely you're not afraid of those bushes,' laughed Kuma, as he tried to regain some of the dignity he had lost the night before.

'It's not the bushes, but what lives in them,' said Kitty. 'We should go no closer.'

Kuma wondered what could be in the bushes and then looked at how far they had come that morning. It was a long way back to the dump should something suddenly chase them. *Does Kitty know that I need rests when I run?* he thought. Then he wondered why he would be running back to the dump anyway. The man with the catch pole was probably waiting for him there. Perhaps no place was safe.

Kuma froze and deep furrows appeared on his brow. This always happened when he had things to think about

'What are you thinking?' Kitty asked.

'Nothing,' said Kuma, suddenly realising that his thoughts were for his own safety and not Kitty's, which was not how a good friend should think. She might have been a monster to the mice, but she was just a small cat that Jock would have loved to have chased.

However, Kitty had noticed something else strange about Kuma's face. 'Did you know that one of your ears is shorter than the other?' she asked.

What a weird time to bring that up, thought Kuma. Danger was close, but she was more interested in his ears.

'No,' he snapped. 'Please tell me what is in those bushes.'

'How could you not know about your ears?' said Kitty, completely ignoring Kuma's question about danger.

'I can't see back there,' Kuma snorted.

'But someone must have told you.'

Kuma glared ahead. 'Stop talking about my ears and tell me what is in the scrub.'

'Just dogs like you,' said Kitty.

'Dogs aren't dangerous,' laughed Kuma.

'These dogs are,' Kitty replied. 'That scrub is home to the Sheep Killer gang. They stalk their victims and strike without warning.'

'Have they tried to catch you?'

'Many times,' she said, 'but I always escape. I'm on their wanted list, and you should be wary too.'

'Why?'

'They might put you on their wanted list if they think you are a friend of mine.'

Suddenly, being friends with Kitty came with danger. Kuma had never been in a dogfight, let alone fought a whole pack of dogs at once. But his mum had taught him that a good dog stays faithful to his friends, and Kitty was his friend. 'How do you escape the Sheep Killers?' he asked.

'Easy,' laughed Kitty. 'I just climb the nearest tree.'

Kuma had felt guilty because his escape plan was only for him. He now discovered that Kitty had her own escape plan, but it was only for her. She had trees to climb, but he would be on his own. 'I can't climb a tree,' he said.

Kitty rolled her eyes. 'That's why we should stay our distance from the scrub.'

'But wouldn't you like us to visit your old home?'

Kitty sighed. 'I have an enemy there who chases me away.'

'Perhaps I could help with that,' said Kuma.

'The Sheep Killers won't let us go through the scrub because it is their territory,' Kitty explained, but then she thought for a moment. 'Perhaps there is a way. We could follow the fence and if the Sheep Killers discover us, I can climb a tree and you can run onto the road. The Sheep Killers don't go near the road.'

'Why?'

'Because farmers patrol the road looking for stray dogs to shoot.'

'What if a farmer shoots me?' Kuma exclaimed.

Kitty frowned. 'Well, no plan is perfect, but it won't be my fault if you get shot. You're the one who won't climb a tree.'

9

ROGER AND BEATRICE

Kuma still wanted to see Kitty's home despite the risks. They continued to follow the fence for it would take them right to the farmhouse gate. A feature of the fence was the tall trees that grew along it. They offered Kitty a safe haven, but Kuma's safety was less assured. Kuma risked being shot should he show himself on the road, and the road ran close to the fence. He had to stay low whenever a car went by.

The two stopped when they reached the scrub, for Kuma needed to overthink things again. The scrub was like the dark, the place where unseen danger lurked. Danger could be hiding behind every bush. Kuma thought about the road, which was also dangerous, but that was a danger he would see. 'Let's walk along the road,' he suggested.

'No,' said Kitty. 'You will be shot if a farmer sees you.'

'You don't know that for sure,' said Kuma.

'I don't think you should push your luck.' said Kitty.

Kuma thought about his luck. Jock had said that Kuma was the unluckiest dog he had ever met. Kuma had been born with unfortunate ears, dumped and made homeless, and then captured by the dogcatcher. Jock had good reason for his opinion, and Kuma's bad luck was yet to change. 'You're right,' he said, 'let's go through the scrub.'

The two began to walk through the bushes, staying as close to the fence as possible. Kuma took note of places where the fence wire was broken, for these were the best places for crawling through to the road. He stayed alert, listening to every sound, and taking in every new fragrance. His senses were seeking danger, but his brain was getting a different message. He was hearing birds and smelling flowers. He was a city dog who had roamed the streets, where tipping a garbage bin had been the highlight of his day. Up until two days ago, he had not known the joy of riding the waves or the peace of walking though natural bushland.

They were almost to the end of their nature walk when they heard human activity. Ahead, was MacLeod. He was fixing part of the fence. With him was his son, Troy, who was home from boarding school for the summer holidays. Troy loved helping his dad and was keen to learn everything that a farmer needed to know. The farm's two kelpies, Seek and Destroy, were there as well. They were sheepdogs, but the challenge posed by the Sheep Killers was one that they were not equipped to handle. They would run whenever the Sheep Killers came near, opting to alert MacLeod rather than face the danger. The kelpies never ventured into the scrub. They had only come that day because humans were with them, and they were staying close to their human protectors.

'We have to go deeper into the scrub to avoid MacLeod,' said Kitty, but then they heard laughter coming from nearby.

A laughing bird was saying, 'You need to go back, little ones, because your mother will be worried where you are.'

'Why is that bird laughing when he says that?' asked Kuma.

'He's a kookaburra, and that's how kookaburras talk,' said Kitty.

They stopped to listen, and then they heard the bleating of lambs. Kitty felt alarm. 'Those lambs shouldn't be in the scrub,' she said. 'If the Sheep Killers hear them, they will be lambs no more. I have to warn them.' She turned and ran toward the bleats.

'What about me?' asked Kuma.

'You're big enough to look after yourself. We are almost out of the scrub. Just keep going but stay out of sight of MacLeod.'

However, Kuma was not letting Kitty out of his sight. He was in a strange place, and wherever she went, he would follow.

They came across two lambs who were frolicking in a clearance. The kookaburra was sitting in a tree and watching over them.

'You can't stay here because the dogs will get you,' Kitty said to the lambs.

'There's a dog right behind you,' laughed the kookaburra.

Don't worry about him,' said Kitty. 'I'm talking about real dogs, not Kuma'

Kuma had suffered many insults in his life, but never had anyone suggested that he was not a real dog. Kuma liked Kitty, but she sometimes said things that hurt his feelings. He was still pondering the insult when the lambs pranced toward him.

'Hello, Mister whatever you are.' said one. 'My name is Beatrice, and this is my brother, Roger.'

'I am a real dog,' growled Kuma. He frowned at Kitty. 'I'm a bullmastiff.'

'Hello, Mr Bullmastiff,' said the lambs in unison.

Hello,' said Kuma. 'My name is Kuma.'

'We are explorers,' explained Roger'

'And we are exploring the jungle,' added Beatrice.

'Actually, they're lost,' laughed the kookaburra. 'I'm here to keep an eye on them.'

Suddenly, a dog appeared. Spike, who was first lieutenant of the Sheep Killers, had also heard the lambs. He was a pitbull who had an ugly scar down the side of his face. The scar was a legacy from a fight with a kangaroo. The fight had left him with only one eye and was the reason the pack had turned to hunting sheep. Prior to that, they had hunted kangaroos, but to date, they had killed neither a sheep nor a kangaroo. Their failures had their leader frustrated.

Spike surveyed the scene as everyone made ready to leave.

'Follow me,' laughed the kookaburra, but Kitty was already running in the direction of the fence. Her plan was to climb one of the taller trees close to the road. Kuma went to follow, but then Kitty shouted, 'You can't follow me because you can't climb trees.'

Kuma was in a situation that they had not anticipated. Kitty's escape plan would work for her, but his plan was in shambles. His plan was to run to the road, but MacLeod would probably see him if he did. He did not know where to run, and he worried about what might happen to the lambs once he left. He froze, and the furrows of thought appeared on his brow. He needed to overthink things again.

The sight of Kuma standing frozen with a strange look on his face, sent a chill of fear down Spike's spine. It was as if Kuma was calmly calculating how best to rip Spike part. Spike considered his options. Does he chase Kitty, does he chase the lambs, or does he pick a fight with odd acting Kuma. Fighting Kuma came last on the list. Spike chose to chase Kitty and hoped that Kuma would not chase him. Spike had a score to settle with that cat, for she had made fools of his gang. Her capture would win him praise from his peers.

With everyone gone, Kuma could think more clearly. He decided to follow the kookaburra.

10

SEEK AND DESTROY

Seek and Destroy were watching the fence being fixed while the lambs' flock grazed in the farmhouse paddock nearby. Suddenly, Seek heard a noise and looked around. 'I think I just saw a lamb run through there,' he said.

'You probably saw a rabbit,' said Destroy. 'No mother would let a lamb stray into the scrub.'

Both dogs peered through the bushes, and they caught a glimpse of Beatrice chasing after her brother. 'See, I did see a lamb, and there goes another one,' said Seek. 'We have to make sure they get back to the flock.'

The dogs rose to their feet, but then they saw Kuma running after the lambs. 'You go,' said Destroy. 'One of us has to stay and supervise the fencing job.'

Neither dog moved. Instead, they both began to howl, which was their way of warning MacLeod that the Sheep Killers were near.

'Can you tell those dogs to shut up,' said MacLeod

'Quiet,' shouted Troy, but the dogs continued to howl.

'That's it, send them home.' MacLeod was not prepared to put up with howling dogs.

'Go home!' growled Troy, but the kelpies stayed put. He whacked Destroy on the rump with his hand. 'Bad dog, go home,' but still they did not move. Troy pushed Destroy with his foot. 'If you don't go home, I will give you both a bath tomorrow.'

A bath was the one thing the kelpies were always keen to avoid. 'I think we should leave,' said Seek. 'It appears that they don't want us to supervise after all.'

The kelpies ran to the edge of the scrub, hoping to get there before more dogs arrived. Ahead, they saw the flock, and in its midst was

Kuma. The kelpies thought that Kuma would be causing panic, but the sheep were acting as if he was one of them.

'What should we do?' asked Seek.

'I reckon the two of us can handle him,' said Destroy, 'but if not, get ready to run.' Destroy cautiously approached Kuma. 'Hey dog, what are you doing with those sheep?'

Kuma looked up, but Beatrice answered the question. 'He's not a dog. He's our friend, Mr Kuma.'

'He looks like a dog to me,' said Destroy. 'I think he's part of the Sheep Killer gang.'

I'm glad that someone thinks I'm a dog, thought Kuma, and then Roger came to his defence.

'Kuma doesn't kill sheep. Kuma is a bullmastiff. Kuma kills bulls.'

'I don't kill anybody,' protested Kuma. 'I am actually trying to become a vegetarian.'

'A vegetarian dog,' laughed Destroy. 'I don't think the world will ever see one of those.'

'Probably not,' said Kuma, 'but it's a reassuring thing to say when you are standing in a flock of sheep.'

Destroy became serious. 'Tell me truthfully, what did you have for your last meal?'

'Fish.'

'You ate fish?'

Kuma frowned. 'Yes, I ate fish, which is almost the same thing as eating a vegetable.'

'Animals like us don't eat fish,' said Destroy.

'My friend, Kitty, eats fish,' said Kuma.

Beatrice interrupted. 'Kitty was with Kuma when he saved us from the one-eyed dog. The one-eyed dog is afraid of Kuma. He ran away.'

Destroy looked at Kuma. 'Are you a friend of Kitty?'

'Yes.'

'And is Spike, the first lieutenant of the Sheep Killers, afraid of you?'

'I don't know who he was,' said Kuma. 'He just looked like an ordinary dog to me, but perhaps that was because he was not wearing his first lieutenant's uniform.'

'Dogs don't wear uniforms,' giggled Beatrice.

The kelpies could see some advantage in having an ally that the Sheep Killers feared. 'Come with us,' said Destroy. 'We will give you some real dog food back at the farmhouse, but you will have to stay out of sight of MacLeod. We will show you how to get there without being seen.'

Kuma followed the kelpies to where the land dipped away at the far side of the paddock. 'We call this the dip,' said Destroy. 'It runs from behind the farmhouse, right to the top of the cliffs. You can walk its full length without being seen from the farmhouse.'

The dogs walked along the dip and stopped when they reached the farmhouse buildings. The kelpies' kennel was behind the barn, and the barn was behind the farmhouse. They trotted up to the kennel and Kuma was shown the kelpies' bowls, which were full of dried dog food. 'They give us so much of this that we get sick of eating it,' said Seek. 'You can come here and help yourself any time you like.'

'You are so kind,' said Kuma, 'but how can I repay you?'

'Is Spike really frightened of you?' asked Destroy.

'I think so.'

'How would you like the job of guarding the sheep? It comes with food and lodgings.'

'Where would I be living?'

The kelpies told Kuma about the old Volkswagen that MacLeod had dumped at the far end of the dip. The vehicle had lost a door and had been stripped of wheels and motor. There was also no windscreen, but it still had seats and had once been Troy's cubby. The car had been dumped close to the cliff top so that Troy could sit in the driver's seat and look out over the sea. He would pretend that he was flying a plane over the ocean.

Kuma thought that living in the Volkswagen would be better than living in the dump, but first, he would have to ask Kitty. *Kitty! I have forgotten all about Kitty,* he thought. *I hope she got up a tree in time.*

'I have to go and ask Kitty,' he said, and then he bolted back down to the dip.

'He seems in a big hurry,' said Seek.

I guess he's excited about our offer,' said Destroy.

11

THE HERO RETURNS

Kuma headed back along the dip and then over the paddock. He passed the sheep who were grazing where he had left them. Beatrice and Roger saw him. 'Hey, Mr Kuma, can we come exploring with you?'

'Not now, kids' barked Kuma, who was in too much of a hurry to stop. He kept running until he reached the scrub, the dreaded place that he had wanted to avoid that morning. He listened and heard noises. MacLeod and Troy were still working on the fence. They were unaware that Kitty was in a nearby tree, trapped by the Sheep Killers who were now gathered at its base. The dogs had come with stealth, which was their way, and only Kitty knew that they were there.

Kuma listened, and the longer he listened, the more frightened he became. He was on his own and thought about turning back, but Milo's words had become etched in his brain. *You must forget your fears if you want to be free.* Kuma knew that guilt would follow him always should he do nothing to help his friend.

Kuma skirted MacLeod by going deeper into the scrub. He crept through the bushes, fearing that unseen danger could be all around him. The breeze was blowing in his face, which was a good thing. He was downwind of whatever lay ahead, and his keen sense of smell should warn him of an ambush. He sniffed the air, hoping to sense a cat, but what he detected was the danger he feared. Ahead were dogs—lots of dogs.

Kuma could tell that the dogs were near the fence and close to where Kitty had run that morning. They were well positioned to cut him off should he run to the road, and the road was his only safe haven should they decide to attack.

He carefully skirted MacLeod and Troy and then crept back to the fence. There he saw Kitty. She was high in a tree, swaying back and

44

forth, and she appeared to be poking out her tongue. Kuma crawled closer, for Kitty was saying something. He wanted to hear.

'Give up, boys,' Kitty was taunting. 'I can stay up here all day, but you have to worry about MacLeod. He's closer than you think.'

Strangely, the dogs were unaware that MacLeod and Troy were nearby. The breeze was coming from the wrong direction, but Kitty could see everything and had been trying to attract MacLeod's attention. She let out another loud meow.

'I just heard that cat again,' said Troy. 'Can I go and see what its problem is?'

'We don't have time to worry about cats,' muttered MacLeod. 'Dogs are our only worry.'

Meanwhile, back under the tree, Spike gave an evil chuckle. 'You won't be escaping this time, cat. No one is coming to save you. We can take shifts and stay here for days. Eventually, you will fall to our feet.'

Sadly, Spike was right, and the dogs would not have much longer to wait. The tree swayed in the breeze, and Kitty was finding it hard to hang on.

Kuma worked his way along the fence until he dared go no closer. Kitty was almost above him, and only a bush separated him from the dogs. He pushed his head through the bush to get a better look. There he saw about a dozen dogs of assorted size and colour, all looking skyward, their eyes fixed on Kitty. However, pushing his head through the bush had not been a good idea. A small flower tickled his nose and he needed to sneeze. He held back, shut his eyes, clenched his teeth, but all to no avail. Nothing could hold back that sneeze. He let out a mighty snort, then a grunt, and then he shook his head. That felt better, but he now had the pack looking at him. 'Get him,' shouted Spike. Kuma pushed through the fence and ran to the road. Fortunately, the dogs stopped at the fence. That was as far as they dared to go.

'Let the idiot go,' snarled Spike. 'There's nothing he can do. I want to get this cat.'

Nearby, MacLeod needed another coil of wire and he asked Troy to fetch it. Troy went back to the truck and looked down the road. 'Hey dad, there's a black dog sitting in the middle of the road.'

MacLeod realised that the dog was most likely the one that he could not shoot the day before. People had ridiculed him ever since. He had failed in his duty, and that dog was now close to his sheep. The sheep's lives were in danger. He went to his truck and grabbed his rifle, then rested it on the truck's open door. He took aim.

Kuma looked down the road and saw MacLeod. Instinct told him to run, but he wondered in what direction. He paused, but fortunately, Kitty could see everything from the tree. *This is not a good time for Kuma to overthink things*, she thought. 'Run, Kuma, run!' she yelled.

'Which way?' Kuma barked.

There was no time for a detailed answer, for Kitty knew that would only confuse Kuma more. 'Over here,' she called, but it was already too late.

MacLeod squeezed the trigger and Kuma's fate seemed sealed, but then an unlikely hero came to Kuma's rescue. A fly crawled into MacLeod's eye, spoiling his aim. The gun fired, but the bullet hit the bitumen and then whistled past Kuma's ear. Kuma thought that he had been hit because he heard a loud smack, but panic prevented him from feeling any pain. He ran toward the fence but slipped on the gravel at the side of the road. He rolled forward just as a second bullet flew past his backside. He crawled through the fence and was once more amid the Sheep Killers. They looked at him and then at Spike. They were waiting for an order. Kuma decided to play dead.

'I think I got him,' yelled MacLeod as he ran toward the motionless Kuma. Kitty could see that playing dead would become the real thing if Kuma did not move. 'Keep running, Kuma,' she yelled. Kuma jumped up and dashed between his bewildered enemies.

'What do we do, boss,' asked a dog.

The sound of the gunfire simplified Spike's decision. 'Scatter,' he barked, just as MacLeod reached the fence.

MacLeod fired a volley of shots, but none hit a scurrying dog. He went to give chase, but then discovered the effectiveness of his own fence. He caught his overalls on the barbed wire as he tried to climb through.

Kuma ran until he could run no more. He stopped and saw several dogs run past him. They were running to safety, but deep in the scrub was not a safe place for Kuma. He was already deep in that realm of unseen danger, and a man with a gun was chasing him. Many times, he had imagined similar nightmares while lying in the dark, but this one was real. He decided to hide in a bush.

12

THE FARM

Kuma remained in the bush for some time, and then he heard a voice. 'You can come out now. They've all gone.' Kitty was standing beside the bush. She had come down from the tree and had been looking for him.

'I think I need to hide here a bit longer,' said Kuma. 'This is a good hiding place. No one will ever find me in here.'

'I just did,' said Kitty.

Kuma thought about that. Hiding was hard for a dog his size. He probably should have chosen a bigger bush. 'I'm sorry I took so long to rescue you,' he said.

Kitty laughed. 'I would hardly call that a rescue. From what I saw, you were mostly running away.'

'And what if I hadn't come back?'

Kitty paused. 'Okay, I suppose you did rescue me in a way.'

'In a way?' Kuma growled. 'I almost got shot saving you,' and then he paused to think. *Wait a minute. I think I did get shot. I should have a bullet hole in me somewhere.* He did a quick audit of his body, head, and limbs, but the only thing of interest was an annoying tingle at the end of his good ear.

'My ear hurts,' he complained.

Kitty looked. 'Which ear, the long one or the short one.'

'The long one.'

Kitty looked again. 'Which is the long one? They both seem to be the same length. Do you mean the one with blood on it?'

'That's the one that hurts,' said Kuma. 'I think I grazed it when I fell on the gravel.'

'That's not a graze,' said Kitty. 'MacLeod has shot a bit of your ear off.'

'Is that why the bullet sounded so loud,' said Kuma, but then he saw the bright side. 'Are you telling me that both my ears are the same length now?'

'They are,' said Kitty.

'Fantastic,' said Kuma. His tail wagged.

'But they aren't the same shape.'

'Oh,' was Kuma's response. His face dropped and his tail stopped wagging.

However, there was no time for them to talk about Kuma's altered appearance. 'We need to go,' said Kitty. 'This place is not safe.' Kuma turned and headed for the farm, which caused Kitty to ask, 'Where are you going? The dump is this way.'

Kuma realised that a lot had happened since he last saw her. They sat back down and Kuma told her about the lambs, the kelpies, the farm, and his new job that came with lodgings in a Volkswagen.

'Did you get to meet Smugs at the farm?' Kitty asked.

'Who's Smugs?'

'Oh, nobody,' said Kitty, sounding rather vague. She did not want to tell Kuma how Smugs had driven her from home. Smugs had come to the farm as a cute, little kitten, but had grown to be a big, selfish cat. Smugs seldom moved far from the farmhouse kitchen window, where she sat all day and demanded everyone's attention. She was jealous of Kitty and had attacked her, telling her to leave the farm and never return.

'I think we should live on the farm,' said Kuma.

Kitty shook her head. 'The farm is not safe.'

'We can hide in the Volkswagen,' Kuma argued.

Kitty shook her head again. 'I can't go back to the farm.'

'Why not?'

'Because I just can't, that's why not.'

'Please,' pleaded Kuma. 'I don't want to sleep on my own. I'm afraid of the dark. You are my best friend. Please come with me. Nothing scares you.'

Kuma had said something that Kitty thought no one would ever say to her. He had called her his best friend. She had never been a best friend before, and Kuma's pleading worked. 'Okay, I will try living in the old car,' she said, hoping that Smugs would never find her there.

The two went back through the paddock and then along the dip. Kuma's tail wagged all the way, but Kitty became wary once they were close to the farmhouse. 'Make sure that no one sees us,' she said.

Kuma thought that Kitty was warning him to stay in the dip so that no one would see him, but Kitty was actually worried about herself. She feared that Smugs would see her from the kitchen window and Smugs was a cat that she wanted to avoid.

'Let's see if Seek and Destroy are home,' said Kuma, and he headed for their kennels.

Seek was lying in the sun while Destroy was chewing on a bone that he had been mauling for the last few days. The kelpies looked up and saw that they had visitors.

'Hi Kitty, we've missed you,' barked Seek.

'We haven't seen you for ages,' barked Destroy. 'Where have you been?'

'Oh, I've been on a holiday at the dump,' Kitty explained. She was ashamed to tell them that Smugs had driven her away.

'I've heard that the dump is a great place for a holiday,' said Seek.

'It is,' said Kitty. 'New attractions keep arriving all the time and fresh food gets delivered every day. A dog like you would never be bored in a place like that, and the night life is fabulous.'

'What night life?' asked Seek.

Kuma rolled his eyes. 'I think she's talking about the mice.'

Seek turned to Kuma. 'Sorry, Kuma, I didn't see you there. We are both just so excited to see Kitty again.'

Fibber, thought Kuma. *No one can miss a dog my size.*

However, Seek felt embarrassed. 'Let me make it up to you,' he said. 'Have some of my dried dog food.'

'You can have my bone if you like,' added Destroy.

Kuma looked at the bone, but Destroy's dribble had taken away its appeal. 'I will just have the dog food thanks,' he said.

Kuma began to eat, which made Kitty think about her food. 'I guess my food bowl has been taken away,' she sighed.

'No,' said Seek. 'It's still in the same place, outside the kitchen window, next to the birdbath. They put food in it every day just in case Smugs decides that she wants to spend some time outside.'

'They put a cat's bowl next to a birdbath?' Kuma asked.

'Humans do things without thinking,' laughed Seek, 'but the birds are safe. Smugs is too well fed to chase them, and Kitty could never be bothered.'

I never do anything without thinking, thought Kuma, but he thought it best not to boast about it.

Kitty wanted to go to her bowl, but she was afraid that Smugs might see her, and she did not want people knowing that she was afraid of Smugs. She chose her words carefully. 'I would like to eat from my bowl,' she said, 'but I'm worried that Smugs might think it is her bowl now. Could someone help me explain things to her if she complains?'

'Not me.' said Seek.

'Nor me,' said Destroy. 'That cat scares me. I think she wants to scratch my eyes out.'

'She spits every time I go past her,' Seek added.

Kitty had never realised that the kelpies were also afraid of Smugs. Perhaps it was time for her to show a little bravery.

The three dogs watched as Kitty crept toward her bowl. They could see Smugs dozing in the kitchen window. Smugs was a grey tabby and was almost twice Kitty's size. *I think I would be afraid of that cat if I were Kitty,* thought Kuma.

The dogs watched Kitty edge closer to her bowl, and sure enough, Smugs opened one eye. What happened next caused Kuma's jaw to drop. Smugs came flying out through a cat flap, screaming, 'I'm going to kill you this time.'

Kitty turned and ran back behind the barn. 'I guess they don't like each other,' Seek said to Destroy, but that was the least of Destroy's worries.

'Run,' he barked, 'before that cat comes back here and kills us.'

The kelpies headed for the dip, but Kuma stood his ground. Kitty took shelter between his legs just as Smugs came flying around the corner. Smugs had to brake to avoid crashing into Kuma, but only her legs stopped. The rest of her kept going. She tumbled headfirst and finished tummy up under Kuma's nose. 'W-who are you?' she spluttered.

'I'm Kitty's friend,' said Kuma, 'but who are you?'

Kitty crouched beneath Kuma, defiantly looking out at Smugs. Smugs was trembling. 'I'm a f-friend of K-kitty too,' she stammered. 'I was just c-coming to tell her that she c-can have some of my f-food if she likes.'

'That's very kind of you,' said Kuma, 'and a friend of Kitty is a friend of mine. You must tell me if you ever see anyone giving Kitty trouble, and I will make it my business to deal with them.'

Smugs got the message and went back to the kitchen window from where she watched Kitty enjoy her finest meal in a week. Kitty was safe from Smugs for as long as Kuma was around.

13

NEW LODGINGS

The kelpies listened from the safety of the dip, puzzled that they were not hearing sounds of battle. 'It sounds very quiet up there,' said Seek.

'Perhaps they're all dead,' said Destroy.

'One of us needs to check.' said Seek.

'You go,' said Destroy.

'Why me?'

'Because it's your idea.'

The kelpies agreed to go together, adopting a safety in numbers policy. They crept back to their kennels and found Kuma eating their dry dog food.

'Where's Smugs?' asked Seek.

'Back in her window,' said Kuma, as a bit of food fell from his mouth. He inspected the morsel as it lay on the ground. It was still partly dirt free. 'Waste not, want not,' he said as he scooped it up with his tongue.

'He's a very messy eater,' whispered Destroy, but Seek had more questions.

'Where's Kitty?'

'Around at her bowl.'

'Is she dead?'

'No.'

'How come?'

'Smugs said she can have as much of her food as she wants.

'Smugs said that?'

'I think everyone on this farm is being very generous,' said Kuma. 'You have offered me a share of your food, and now Smugs is doing the same for Kitty.'

'I guess people do nice things for a dog his size,' whispered Destroy.

'Shush,' said Seek.

Kitty finished her meal and returned to chat with the kelpies, which gave Kuma time for a rest. He stretched out for a while, and then he was ready for Kitty to show him their new home. They bid the kelpies farewell and headed along the dip, for the Volkswagen lay where the dip ended at the cliff top. They arrived and heard bleating coming from inside the car. Through the entrance that was always open because the Volkswagen had no driver's door, they saw Beatrice and Roger playing on the seats. 'What are you guys doing here?' Kuma asked.

'This is our cubby,' said Beatrice. 'It's our secret place that no one knows about. We discovered it when we were exploring.'

'That's the advantage of being explorers,' said Roger. 'We discover places that no one knows about.'

Kitty smiled, for she had known about the Volkswagen long before the lambs were born, but she said nothing. 'Can we come in?' she asked.

'Certainly,' said Beatrice.

The lambs stepped aside, and Kuma hopped in, keen to test the comfort of the back seat. 'I've found my bed,' he said, and then he looked through the space where there had once been a windscreen. 'This bedroom comes with an excellent view of the sea,' he added.

The Volkswagen was close to the cliff top, but it was protected from the wind because it lay within the dip. The only sound to be heard was the waves lapping on the beach. The place was so peaceful. Kuma thought that nothing bad could ever happen to him here.

'Pass inspection?' said Kitty.

'I've moved in already, 'said Kuma. He settled onto the back seat and shut his eyes.

'Hey, don't go to sleep, Mr Kuma,' bleated Beatrice. 'We want to play.'

Kuma groaned.

'Come on,' said Kitty, 'playing will do you good. You need to get rid of your surplus weight.'

'It's puppy fat,' snorted Kuma.

'I know,' said Kitty, 'and you need to act like a puppy until you get rid of it.'

'Is Mr Kuma a puppy?' giggled Beatrice.

'Does that mean we can call him Kuma and not Mr Kuma?' added Roger.

'No,' growled Kuma.

'Call him Kuma,' said Kitty, 'because you two will probably be sheep long before he becomes an adult.'

Kuma pretended not to hear.

The foursome frolicked together for some time. First, Roger would chase Beatrice, and then Beatrice would chase Roger. Next, there would be a challenge to see who could jump highest over a clump of grass. After that, Kitty would hide from the lambs and then leap out whenever one came her way. Kuma made himself into a ramp, allowing the lambs to run up his back and jump off his head. At other times, Kuma would stand, and Kitty would use his tail as a swinging rope.

The games ended when the kelpies made a surprise visit. They had been looking for the lambs because their mother had reported them missing.

'You naughty lambs have to come back to the safety of the flock,' barked Seek.

'But we are safer here with Kuma,' pleaded Beatrice. 'He can protect us.'

The kelpies thought for a moment. Beatrice was right. They were safer with Kuma. 'Stay here then,' said Seek, 'we have an idea.'

The kelpies bounded away, and everyone went back to their games. However, a short time later they heard *baa*, followed by more *baas,* and then they heard a chorus of non-stop *baas.* Kuma ran to the crest of the dip. The kelpies were bringing the flock to them.

14

KUMA'S NEW JOB

The day ended peacefully with the sheep dozing close to the Volkswagen. They felt safe, knowing that their guardian was close by, ready to leap into action if needed. However, their guardian's only thought was to get a good night's sleep, but his ear was sore. Kitty had been licking it whenever she had the chance, for her mother had told her that licking a wound was the best way to make it heal.

'I wish I could lick my own ear,' said Kuma. 'Your tongue is a bit rough.'

'Stop complaining,' said Kitty. 'My mother told me that I would make a good nurse.'

'Are my ears really a different shape?' Kuma asked.

'Yes.'

'Do they make me look horrible?'

Kitty answered carefully, for she knew that Kuma's feelings were easily hurt. 'No,' she said. 'Your ears just make you look interesting, like a pirate who has seen many battles.'

Kuma was not convinced. 'Do you think I should wear a hat?'

'Dogs don't wear hats,' laughed Kitty, but then she asked, 'Do you want to wear a hat?'

Kuma thought back to some pampered pooches he had seen in the city, and he was sure that one of them had worn a hat. He remembered that it looked rather silly. He shook his head. 'No. I won't wear a hat because I can't see myself, and how I look is someone else's problem, not mine. I will just tell them that I'm a pirate.'

Kuma fell asleep, but later that night, he was woken by a noise. It had been twilight when he had last looked out, but it was now the dead of night. He listened and heard Spike's voice coming from somewhere outside. He needed to wake Kitty, but she was already awake. She was looking out with her keen, night vision, and she could see the Sheep

Killers. They were assembling, one by one, at the top of the cliff. 'I need to tell the kelpies,' she said.

'I will go with you,' whispered Kuma.

'No, you have to stay and protect the sheep. It's your job. Beatrice and Roger are relying on you.'

Kitty ran off, leaving Kuma to wonder about the terms of his employment. The conditions were good, namely free food and accommodation, but the duties had never been properly explained. *Did I really agree to fight the Sheep Killers?* he thought. *I think I'm being underpaid.*

The Sheep Killers crawled toward the Volkswagen, from where they planned to rush the sheep. Kuma clenched his teeth, 'Grrrr.'

'Who said that?' said Spike.

'None of us,' came a reply.

Spike hesitated. He was the one in front. The rest were behind him. *Who was in the car?*

'Grrrr,' Kuma snarled again.

'I want two of you to check inside the car,' Spike ordered. 'You and you—go.'

'Why us, boss? Why not him and him?'

'Go!'

The two dogs crawled on their bellies and then paused by the Volkswagen. 'Get in there and look,' snarled Spike.

The first dog poked his head into the cabin and bumped his nose on the steering wheel. Kuma leant over the driver's seat and sunk his teeth into the intruder's neck. There was one mighty yelp. The dog writhed and kicked but could not escape Kuma's vice like grip. Kuma threw him out the door.

The other dog saw his friend being flung across the ground. 'Run for your lives, there's a monster in the car,' he yelped.

'Stay where you are,' snapped Spike. 'A monster could not fit into that car,' but then he heard the kelpies bark. Kitty had raised the alarm and the kelpies were alerting MacLeod. Spike's raid on the sheep had been thwarted. 'Retreat,' he ordered.

'I'm glad the boss changed his mind,' a dog mumbled.

Kuma had thought that the gully offered the only way down to the beach, but he was about to learn another. A goat track started where the dip met the cliff top, and it ran diagonally down the cliff face. It was the way the Sheep Killers had come and was now their path of retreat. They retreated in single file, down a narrow walkway where one false step would see them fall.

Kuma's eyes were just becoming accustomed to the dark as the last of the dogs disappeared over the cliff. He ran to where the dog had been and saw the pack working its way down to the beach. Meanwhile, Kitty was bringing the rescue squad. Troy was driving the truck with MacLeod standing on the back. MacLeod was holding his rifle and spotlight, and Kitty was bounding behind. However, the kelpies stayed in their kennels. They decided to wait until morning for news of the night's happenings.

Troy stopped the truck close to the flock, but he needed to have gone further to see the escaping dogs. 'The killers are over here,' barked Kuma, but the humans did not understand dog language. MacLeod shone the spotlight and saw Kuma standing at the edge of the cliff. He raised his rifle but found it difficult to shoot and hold the spotlight at the same time. He fired, and a puff of dust burst from the ground next to Kuma's paw.

I'm definitely being underpaid, thought Kuma. He followed the Sheep Killers' lead and stepped over the cliff, placing a nervous paw on the goat track. It was dark. He had to feel his way down. One false step would see him fall to a probable death. The spotlight's beam shone above him, harmlessly aimed out to sea, but MacLeod was almost at the cliff top. The spotlight would soon be lighting up the cliff face. Kuma was about to become an easy target.

MacLeod got to the cliff top and shone his light onto the beach, hoping to see a dead dog. 'He has to be down there somewhere,' he shouted. 'I'm sure I shot him this time.'

Kuma was only moments from being discovered when he came to a place that offered safety. Part way down the goat track was a slight hollow in the cliff face, and within it was a ledge on which he could stand. Kuma stood on the ledge and pushed his body hard into the hollow just as the spotlight's beam swept past. He escaped detection.

MacLeod swept the beam back along the beach and caught the last of the Sheep Killers making their escape. 'Damn,' he said, 'but at least the kelpies sounded the alarm and saved the sheep. Remind me to give them their favourite meal tomorrow,' but he was not happy. That black dog had foiled him again. He wondered about its elusiveness and cunning. It had to be the Sheep Killers' leader.

15

IN TROUBLE AGAIN

The rest of the night was uneventful. The truck headed back to the farmhouse and Kitty and Kuma went back to bed. They slept until morning, and then were woken by the lambs kicking on the side of the car.

'Get up you two, we want to play,' bleated Roger.

Kuma shook his head. His ear still hurt, and he wanted more sleep. 'How come you guys are up so early,' he grumped. 'We had a terrible night.'

'We had a good night's sleep,' bleated Beatrice. 'Last night was so peaceful. All the sheep had a good night's sleep.'

'You didn't hear a fight, or a truck, or a gun going off.'

'No.'

'Really?' Kuma was puzzled.

'You must have been having a bad dream,' said Beatrice.

Kuma looked at Kitty. 'Was last night a dream?'

'No,' she said. 'I think sheep have short memories, which is why they keep making the same mistakes.'

'Not us,' said Beatrice.

'Let's do some more exploring,' said Roger. The lambs said goodbye and bounded away.

Kuma and Kitty headed for the farmhouse and were greeted with great enthusiasm. The kelpies had become heroes because they had saved the sheep by alerting MacLeod. They had been given a special breakfast as their reward.

'Got any left?' asked Kuma.

'We saved you some,' said Seek, because we know that you and Kitty were the real heroes, but we had no way of telling MacLeod that.'

Kitty checked Smugs' bowl, but it only had leftovers from the day before. She ate them but still felt hungry, and so she came looking for dog food. Kitty actually liked dog food, but the dog-size pieces were hard to fit in her mouth. Kuma grabbed some pellets and crushed them for her. 'I would rather have some of the kelpie's special breakfast that you are eating,' she said.

Kuma frowned, but he suspected all along that she would want a share of the special breakfast. 'Help yourself,' he mumbled.

They were eating the last of the special meal when a visitor arrived. The kookaburra, who kept watch over the lambs, had some alarming news. The lambs were in trouble. The Sheep Killers had them cornered and there was no escape.

Everyone followed the kookaburra, but he did not know that Kuma had to travel along the dip. He took a shorter way, which was in full view of the farmhouse. Kitty bounded ahead, but Kuma held back, while the kelpies trailed at the rear. Troy looked out the window and saw the strange procession. 'Hey, dad, the Sheep Killers' leader is back. He's chasing Kitty, and the kelpies are chasing him.'

'Those kelpies are the best dogs we've ever had,' said MacLeod. 'I don't know another sheepdog that would chase a brute like that.' He thought about getting his gun, but it was Sunday. He was in his best suit, making ready to go to church. Sunday was not a day for shooting dogs. 'The kelpies will see him gone,' he said. However, the kelpies soon gave up the chase and returned to their kennels. They were heroes already and could rest on their laurels.

The kookaburra flew on and landed on the Volkswagen's roof. He pointed to a dog hunched at the top of the cliff. The dog was looking down, but he raised his head when he heard them arrive. Kuma realised at once that the dog was Spike.

Kuma had thought that the Volkswagen was in a peaceful place where nothing bad could ever happen, but he did not know that the Sheep Killers also considered it the perfect place to trap their victims. Their idea was for Spike to chase a sheep along the dip until it reached the cliff top. The sheep would then have nowhere to go other than down the goat track to where the rest of the pack was waiting on the beach.

Kuma could hear Spike snarling at a victim on the goat track, and then he heard a bleat.

'Is that you, Beatrice and Roger,' Kuma woofed.

Yeeees,' came a terrified bleat.

Spike snarled. 'Keep out of this, dog. What is happening here is none of your business.' He fixed his one good eye on Kuma and bared his teeth. Then he howled to his gang who were gathered on the beach below. 'Get ready, fellas, I'm sending them down.' With that, he edged down the goat track. The lambs were huddled a short distance away on the same ledge that had saved Kuma the night before.

Kuma ran to the top of the track and could see what was about to happen. If he did nothing, the lambs were doomed.

'Help,' bleated Beatrice, who froze as Spike edged closer.

For the second time in his life, Kuma was filled with rage. The last time had been Milo's fault, but this time, Spike was to blame.

Kuma followed Spike down the goat track, which was too narrow for Spike to turn around. Spike's steps were cautious, but Kuma's were bold. He gained ground until Spike's butt was almost in his face. Meanwhile, Spike's focus was on the lambs, unaware of the danger coming from behind.

'There's that dog behind you,' came a bark from the beach, but the warning came too late.

Kuma sunk his teeth into Spike's butt and almost lifted its owner off the track. Spike let out a pain-filled yowl and then went flying through the air. Kuma watched him fall, and the further he fell, the smaller he seemed to be. The yowl also seemed to fade as impact grew near. However, a bush saved Spike from a fatal fall. He landed in a boxthorn bush growing at the base of the cliff.

'The pack ran to the boxthorn. 'Are you all right in there, boss?'

'Get me out of here,' came the feeble reply.

'We can't, boss.'

'Why?'

'Too many prickles.'

Spike extracted himself from the bush, but branches hung from his body, held in place by imbedded thorns. 'Get these branches off me you idiots,' he growled.

Kuma looked down from the cliff and felt some respect for his enemy. *That is one very tough dog,* he thought. He then made his way down to the ledge and gently took Beatrice in his jaws. He carried her to the top of the cliff and then rescued Roger the same way.

16

A SNAKE IN THE GRASS

Kitty joined Kuma and they sat on the cliff top, watching the Sheep Killers as they made a slow retreat along the beach. Spike hobbled at the rear, his nose almost dragging in the sand.

'I don't think they will be bothering us now that their leader is out of action,' laughed Kuma.

'I think things will get worse,' said Kitty. 'Spike is only their second in command. You haven't met Bruno yet.'

'Who's Bruno?'

Kitty stared toward the retreating dogs. 'Bruno is a dog that you don't want to meet. I haven't seen him for a while, but I'm sure he'll be back. Sometimes, he goes to his old hunting ground where he and Spike used to hunt kangaroos.'

'What breed of dog is he?' asked Kuma

'He's nothing like you,' said Kitty. 'He is a mixture of many breeds and twice your size. His coat is shaggy, grey, and his eyes are evil. If you see him, you must run. When Bruno hears what you have done to Spike, he will want revenge. Your life will be in danger.'

Kuma could not imagine a dog twice his size. *I am the biggest dog I have ever met,* he thought, but that did not sound right. *I have never met a dog as big as me.* That sounded better. Kuma always over thought things when he found himself under stress, and Kitty had just told him that his life was in danger. Kuma felt stressed.

The lambs ran back down the goat track and stood on the ledge.

'How come they are doing that?' said Kuma. 'I had to carry them up not long ago. I thought they would be too frightened to walk back down again.'

'I told you,' said Kitty. 'Sheep have short memories.'

The lambs could hear the conversation from the ledge. 'Thanks for saving us, Kuma,' bleated Roger.

'You are my hero,' added Beatrice.

At least they remember that I saved them, thought Kuma.

Kuma felt honoured, for no one had ever called him a hero before. He thought that he had been a hero when he saved Kitty from the Sheep Killers. He had been shot performing that heroic deed, but she had said that he was running away. Fortunately, the lambs were far more generous with their praise. 'What are you playing?' he asked them.

'We are not playing,' said Roger. 'We are explorers, and explorers need a lookout. This is our lookout where we look out to sea.'

'What do you see out to sea?' laughed Kuma.

'We see fishing boats and sometimes we see a big trawler.'

Kuma's heart skipped a beat when he heard the word trawler. It had to be Jason's trawler. 'Could you tell me the next time you see the trawler,' he asked.

'Sure will,' said Roger, and then he turned to his sister. 'I told you that being an explorer is important work, and now we have an important job to do. One day, we will be famous.'

Kitty frowned. 'You shouldn't be encouraging them, Kuma. You should be telling them how dangerous the ledge is because they have already forgotten.'

Kuma shrugged, 'I don't see the point if they forget all the time. They will just forget that I told them. Playing on the ledge might be dangerous, but it's what they want to do. Sometimes you have to forget your fears if you want to be free.'

Kitty looked at Kuma. She could not believe that he had said that, and ironically, neither could Kuma.

Kuma settled in the long grass that grew at the top of the cliff. His plan was to spend the day helping the lambs to look out for the trawler. Kitty decided to go back to the Volkswagen. Her plan was to catch up on the sleep she had missed the night before.

'I am glad that cat has gone,' came a voice from someone in the grass.

Kuma looked around but saw no one. 'Did someone just speak?' he asked as he wondered if someone invisible was talking to him.

'I am down here,' said the voice. 'I'm a snake. You almost trod on me before.'

'Where are you?'

'Next to your hind leg.'

Kuma stood up and turned around. A small, brown head with two tiny eyes was looking up at him.

'Hello,' said the snake. 'My name is Simon.'

Kuma had never met a snake, but his mother had warned him never to run in long grass because a snake might get him. This had led him to believe that a snake was a fearsome creature that hid in long grass and devoured bullmastiffs, but then Kitty told him not to worry about snakes. She said that snakes were usually in bed. Being an optimist, Kuma liked Kitty's description better because a bed-ridden snake could do him no harm. 'Why aren't you in bed?' he asked Simon.

'Because snakes like to lie in the sun,' came the reply.

The snake's head was no bigger than that of a mouse. 'Are you a baby snake?' asked Kuma.

'No, I'm full grown.' Simon twitched the end of his tail.

Kuma saw the grass move a short distance away. 'There's something back there in the grass behind you,' he warned.

'No, that's just more of me,' said Simon. 'I'm moving my tail to show you how long I am.' He slid out of the grass so that Kuma could see all of him. 'See, I'm bigger than you think.'

'Show me how tall you are when you stand up?' Kuma asked.

'I am standing up,' growled Simon. 'This is how tall I am. People can be so insensitive. It's not my fault that I was born without legs.'

'I'm sorry,' said Kuma, 'but I hadn't noticed. I thought everyone was born with legs. Now I understand why Kitty said that snakes spend a lot of time in bed. Where is your bed, by the way?'

'My bed is under the Volkswagen, but I'm only there at night. Snakes get out in the fresh air during the day, the same as everyone else.'

'The Volkswagen is where I live too,' said Kuma. 'I'm your upstairs neighbour and you have to meet Kitty because she also lives upstairs.' Kuma let out a loud woof. 'Hey Kitty, come and meet our neighbour, Simon.'

'I don't want to meet Kitty,' said Simon. 'Kitty has a bad reputation. Kitty kills snakes.' He slid back into the grass.

Kitty wandered out from the Volkswagen. 'Who's Simon?' she said, still half-asleep.

'Simon is my new friend,' explained Kuma. 'He's a snake, but he says that you have a bad reputation.'

'Snakes are always spreading bad rumours about me,' Kitty scoffed. 'I only ever bit one snake. He was too close to the farmhouse, and when I asked him to leave, he got mad and tried to bite me.'

'That was George,' said Simon, who was listening close by. 'She killed him.'

'Simon says that you killed a snake called George,' said Kuma.

'I had to grab George behind the neck to stop him biting me,' protested Kitty.

'Did you kill him?' asked Kuma.

'I don't know. I just left him at the back door of the farmhouse.'

Kitty was grumpy. She hated being woken from a deep sleep and being accused of murder added to her grumpiness.

'He was dead,' said Simon. 'Ask her if George was still breathing when she left him.'

Kuma was in the middle of a dispute that had nothing to do with him. He hesitated, but then Simon insisted that he ask the question.

Kuma frowned. 'How was George when you left him?'

'Sleeping peacefully,' growled Kitty.

'See Simon, she left him there asleep.'

Kuma hoped that would end the argument, but Simon was not convinced. 'We only have her word for that. Can she prove that he wasn't dead?'

Kuma had had enough. He wanted them both to be friends. He became annoyed. 'Look Simon, whatever happened to George was his own fault. Kitty was only trying to teach him a lesson. I want you both to be friends.'

Simon changed his attitude and laughed. 'That's okay by me. None of us liked George anyway. Besides, after hearing the rumours about Kitty, I would rather be her friend than her enemy.' Simon came out of hiding.

'Let's display our gestures of friendship,' said Kuma

Kuma wagged his tail and Kitty meowed. They looked at Simon. 'Sorry,' he said, 'but I don't know what to do. Snakes don't have a gesture of friendship.'

'We understand,' said Kitty. 'It must be very hard for a snake to appear friendly.'

'True,' said Simon.

The trio spent the morning resting at the cliff top. They looked out over the sea and watched the lambs at play. It was a perfect way for three unlikely creatures to get to know each other.

17

THE MAGIC WORD

It was close to noon when Kuma heard the distant squawking of gulls. He looked toward the ruckus and saw a flock hovering in the air. Below was a creature, thrashing in the water, and Kuma recognised that creature. The unsociable dog, who had caused Kuma to be a castaway, was doing his best to upset the gulls.

'I'm going down there to tell that unsociable dog the trouble he has caused me,' said Kuma.

Simon raised his head to look. 'I wouldn't bother,' he said.

'Why not?'

'He's drowning. He will be dead soon. People don't care what you say to them once they are dead.'

'That's a very cold-blooded thing to say,' said Kitty.

'I can't help it,' said Simon. 'I'm a cold-blooded creature. Snakes are born cold-blooded.' He rested his head back down on the ground.

Kitty was having trouble warming to Kuma's new friend, but Kuma was more concerned about the drowning dog. 'I have to rescue him,' he said.

'Can you swim?' asked Kitty.

'I don't know, but mum said that all dogs can dogpaddle.'

'Have you ever dogpaddled?'

'No.'

With that said, Kuma set out to perform another heroic deed. He dashed down the goat track showing no fear of falling. Next, he charged along the beach. He felt confident that he could rescue the drowning dog because the dog was drowning close to shore, but when he arrived upon the scene he stopped, for he had to think.

What do I do now? he wondered.

Dogpaddle out to the unsociable dog, he told himself.

Do I know how to dog paddle? he thought.

Mum said I can, he answered.

But what about the other question? The furrows on his brow deepened. He was now in full overthinking mode.

How do I drag the unsociable dog back to shore?

I have no idea, was the answer, and at that point his body froze.

Kuma wanted to be a hero but did not know what to do. The unsociable dog was an excellent swimmer, yet Simon said that he was drowning. Kuma could not understand how an excellent swimmer could drown. *Is the unsociable dog just doing things to annoy the gulls,* he thought, because annoying the gulls would be the type of thing an unsociable dog would do. He decided to ask a question. 'Are you alright out there?' he woofed.

'Help me, I'm drowning,' honked the unsociable dog.

Kuma would have preferred the answer to have been, 'I'm annoying the seagulls, so go away,' but that was not the case. 'I don't know how to help you,' Kuma barked.

'Pull in the net,' honked the unsociable dog, who was splashing alongside of a row of corks floating in the water.

'What do you mean?'

A seagull landed on the beach. 'He means drag the net in because he is stuck in it, dimwit. That's the thing next to you. One end is tied to that anchor on the beach and the other end is out there where he is.'

Kuma would have liked to be friends with the seagulls, but to be called a dimwit just added to the insults they were always giving him. 'What good will pulling the net in do?' he asked.

The unsociable dog answered the question. 'My flipper is caught in the net.'

Kuma did not know what a flipper was or why a dog would have one in the water. Obviously, the unsociable dog had lost his flipper in the net, but he was probably pretending to drown so that people would help him get it back. Kuma no longer felt like being a hero. The unsociable dog was just adding to his list of unsociable acts. However, there was a chance that the dog was drowning. Kuma had to find out one way or the other, but he had to do it without losing face. 'I will pull in the net if you say please,' he woofed.

'PLEASE!' honked the unsociable dog.

Kuma had hoped not to hear the magic word, for he was ready to leave, but hearing the magic word meant that he had to stay. He took the net in his jaws and began dragging it up the beach, a section at a time. With each drag, the unsociable dog came a little closer to shore, but then Kuma got distracted. There were fish gilled in the net, and Kuma had never seen a live fish before. He stopped pulling on the net and sniffed one.

'Could you please keep pulling in the net,' honked the unsociable dog.

'Yes, keep pulling the net,' squawked the gulls, 'and keep away from our fish. We know who you are. They call you the fish thief. You steal fish from the beaks of honest seagulls.'

In three days, Kuma had gone from unknown castaway to public enemy number one. The townsfolk hated him; MacLeod hated him; the Sheep Killers hated him, and the seagulls hated him. The unsociable dog was still an unknown, but he guessed that he probably hated him as well. He was doing his best to have people like him, but everyone just kept on hating him. He was fed up with the lot of them. 'I won't pull the net anymore until everyone says please,' Kuma growled. He was not going to be pushed around anymore.

'Everyone say please, or I'm going to drown,' gasped the unsociable dog.

'Please,' squawked the gulls.

The gulls' response surprised Kuma, and it made him feel a little more kindly toward them. He kept pulling on the net. Finally, it was all on the beach and so was the unsociable dog, but part of him was stuck in the net. However, Kuma could not work out what type of a part it was because the unsociable dog had something in common with Simon. Both had been born without legs. The unsociable dog was a cripple who had to waddle on four flat stumps. Kuma felt sympathy, for people had treated him badly because of his odd ears, but that was nothing compared to a dog born with no legs and no ears at all. 'I'm so sorry to see that you were born with such deformities,' he said.

The unsociable dog looked at Kuma with astonishment. 'There is nothing wrong with me. I am perfect in every way, and it surprises me that someone with weird ears would say such a thing.'

Kuma's sympathy evaporated. 'I might have weird ears, but you are weird all over. You look like no dog that I have ever met.'

'That's because I'm not a dog. I'm a seal, and seals have flippers, not legs. I also have tiny ears if you look hard enough.'

'Why would a seal have flippers?' Kuma asked.

A seagull interrupted. 'For swimming with you dumbo, and we can't believe that you would refuse to rescue a drowning person until they said please.'

The seagull had called Kuma a dumbo after he had just caught them a feed of fish. The kindly feelings he was beginning to have for them, were no more. He would never do another favour for a seagull, and he now knew why dogs always chased them at the beach. However, he did owe the seal an apology. Asking the drowning seal to say please was not the action of a hero. 'I'm sorry for asking you to say please,' he said.

The seal frowned. 'You also said that I looked weird.'

'I'm sorry for that too,' said Kuma. 'Can I help you get out of that net?'

Strangely, so upset was the seal with Kuma, that he had forgotten that he was still stuck in the net. However, Kuma was now saying sorry, and sorry was another magic word.

'Apology accepted,' said the seal, 'My name is Ralph, and I would greatly appreciate any help you can give.'

'I'm glad to meet you,' said Kuma. 'My name is Kuma.'

Kuma gripped the net close to Ralph's flipper and yanked with all his might.

'Ouch, that hurts,' honked Ralph. 'Haven't you got some better way of doing it?'

Kuma thought for a moment. 'Perhaps I could chew your flipper off.'

'NO!'

'Just joking.'

However, Ralph's problems were about to get worse.

18

BRUNO RETURNS

Kuma and Ralph tried in vain to cut the net with their teeth, but then the seagulls squawked a warning. 'The fisherman is coming.'

Ralph's life was in danger, for the fisherman had his own method of removing a seal from his net, and that involved a heavy club. Ralph became frantic. 'Help me, help me,' he honked.

'I am helping,' barked Kuma.

'Help me more,' honked Ralph, but sadly, Kuma could do no more.

'How about you guys help us,' Kuma barked to the gulls.

'What can we do?' came a reply.

'Swoop the fisherman or something.'

A seagull walked up to Kuma and stood with wings on hip. 'We don't do the magpie thing. We are far too respectable for that.'

'I hate seagulls,' said Kuma.

'Me too,' said Ralph.

They each grabbed the net in their teeth and began pulling in opposite directions.

'Look, fellas, a tug of war,' squawked a gull. 'Let's pick sides.'

Some gulls chanted, 'Ralph, Ralph, Ralph,' while others chanted, 'Kuma, Kuma, Kuma.'

The fisherman's boat was now close to the beach and the sight of squawking gulls had him excited. It could mean only one thing. His net was full of fish. He ran the bow of his boat up onto the sand, but then his excitement turned to anger. His net had been pulled out of the water and the culprits were now using it for tug of war. He grabbed a wooden club and strode towards them.

'He wants to play fetch,' said Kuma, 'but I wish he had a smaller stick.'

'That stick is for me, not you,' exclaimed a trembling Ralph. 'He's going to bash me with it.'

Kuma glared at the fisherman in disbelief. Only a dogcatcher would do such a thing, and Kuma hated dogcatchers even more than he hated seagulls. He looked at Ralph and saw the fear in his eyes. The fisherman was acting like a dogcatcher.

'We have to forget our fears if we want to be free,' Kuma barked, and then he stood between Ralph and the fisherman. 'Grr,' he snarled.

The fisherman stepped back. 'Nice doggy, nice doggy.'

Kuma lunged at the club and ripped it from the fisherman's hand. The fisherman turned to run back to the boat, but Kuma blocked his path. They stood frozen, each staring at the other. Kuma needed time to think, but then a plan flashed into his head. It was a good plan, but it did have a flaw. He would have to speak human.

Kuma stepped forward and the fisherman stepped back. Kuma took another step forward, and again, the fisherman stepped back. Finally, the fisherman was almost beside Ralph. The plan was working, but now came the part where he had to speak human.

Kuma ran around the fisherman and pushed his snout against Ralph's flipper. He then looked up at the fisherman and wagged his tail. 'Woof,' he said.

The fisherman made another dash for the boat, but Kuma cut him off. Again, Kuma forced the fisherman back to where Ralph was trapped, and again he nudged Ralph's flipper and wagged his tail. 'Woof,' he repeated.

This time, the fisherman understood. 'You want me to free the seal's flipper?' he said.

'Woof,' Kuma barked, and then he nodded.

The fisherman drew a knife from his belt. Kuma frowned a warning. 'Grrr.'

The fisherman looked at Kuma. 'It's okay, I'm just going to cut the net.'

Kuma watched the fisherman's every move, and Ralph was soon cut free.

Ralph hastily shuffled back to the water. Once safe, he looked back. 'Thanks for saving me, Kuma. You're a hero,' he honked. He waved his wounded flipper and then swam out to sea.

Ralph's praise had left Kuma satisfied with his morning's work. He had befriended the unsociable dog, talked the human language, and confirmed his status as a hero. However, none of this seemed to be impressing the gulls, and Kuma heard one say, 'Nothing interesting happening here, fellas. Let's head back to town and hang about outside the fish and chips shop.'

The fisherman began to gather his net. 'Can I help?' woofed Kuma, but there was nothing that a dog could do. 'Can I come for a ride when you are finished?' he asked, but the fisherman ignored him. It seemed that Kuma had already lost his ability to speak human.

However, close by was someone who understood exactly what Kuma was saying. Bruno was returning to the pack after being away for a few days. He had been walking along the beach when he had seen Ralph's plight. Bruno knew what the fisherman did to seals, and he had decided to hide a short distance away. An injured seal left lying on the beach would be an easy kill for him, but Kuma had foiled his plan.

Bruno emerged from behind a bush at the base of the cliff and bared his fangs. 'I know you,' he snarled at Kuma. 'I received a message yesterday, telling me that a cat lover was giving my boys trouble. You are the coward who attacked my first lieutenant when he wasn't looking, and you threw him into a prickle bush.'

The fisherman panicked at the sight of Bruno and made retreat his priority. The net was left where it lay, for the fisherman had never seen a creature so frightening. He did not know if Bruno was a grey lion or an oversized wolf, but either way, Bruno could well be a man-eater.

The fisherman pushed the boat off the sand and pointed its bow seaward. He jumped on board and started the motor, but then he felt the boat jolt. Something heavy had landed behind him. He turned in fear and saw Kuma. He was coming too. 'Hurry, before that dog gets here,' Kuma barked.

To Kuma's delight, the fisherman did as instructed. *Yes, I can speak human after all,* he thought.

The fisherman engaged drive and the boat headed out to sea, leaving an enraged Bruno standing on the beach. Abandoned were the fisherman's club and net. They were left lying on the sand, and Kuma wondered what danger the fisherman posed now that he no longer had his club. Similarly, the fisherman was worried about Kuma, for the Fisherman's only choice should Kuma attack him, was to jump over the side.

'Good doggy,' said the fisherman.

Kuma wagged his tail. The fisherman gave him a cautious pat. Kuma wagged his tail again and then jumped onto the bow. 'Go faster, go faster,' he woofed.

What a crazy dog, thought the fisherman, *but at least he now seems friendly.*

The fisherman was soon able to relax because Kuma was in a world of his own. The boat was like the trawler, only smaller. Kuma stood on its front deck and watched each oncoming wave. He felt the bow lift and then crash, and he barked at the spray as it was pushed to the sides. He was reliving his last adventure at sea.

19

WANTED DEAD OR ALIVE

The fisherman was having a bad day, for he had been forced to leave his net on the beach and the gulls had eaten his catch. However, he had seen a new poster in town, and he knew a way to turn his bad fortunes around. The unsuspecting Kuma was in far more danger than he realised, because the poster bore the picture of a black bullmastiff, and it read:

WANTED, DEAD OR ALIVE.
The leader of the Sheep Killers
REWARD $100.

However, the picture was not one of Kuma, because no one had ever taken a picture of Kuma. The picture was that of another bullmastiff, but that did not matter, for Kuma was the only black bullmastiff in the district.

The boat motored into the jetty and the fisherman called to a young lad watching over some crab nets. 'I will give you a dollar if you run home and fetch me a dog leash.'

'Why do you want a dog leash?' asked the young crabber.

'I've captured the leader of the Sheep Killers, and I need to have him on a leash when I take him ashore.'

'Is that the dog that has a hundred bucks on his head?'

'Yes.'

'In that case, it's going to cost you five bucks.'

'Okay, five bucks, but no more.'

The young crabber ran home, leaving the fisherman to think unkind thoughts about the younger generation. A short time later, the lad was back with a red dog leash, and behind him were many of the townsfolk. News of the outlaw's capture was spreading like wildfire.

The young crabber threw the leash into the boat, and Kuma soon found it attached to his collar. The fisherman restarted the motor and

Kuma let out an excited woof. He was about to have another boat ride, but he wondered about the leash. He guessed that it had been attached for his own safety. The thoughtful fisherman wanted something to grab should Kuma fall overboard. But alas, Kuma's expectations were soon dashed, because the journey was short. The boat ran onto the beach alongside the jetty.

Kuma looked up and saw a crowd waiting to welcome him. He was bemused at first, but then he recognised some as having wished him harm the last time he was in town. *This is not good,* he thought. *I think I will stay on the boat,* but he was given no choice. The fisherman jumped ashore and gave the leash a sharp tug, and Kuma found himself back on dry land.

'I need to run up to the cop shop and report the capture of the wanted dog,' shouted the fisherman. 'Can someone hold the dog here until I get back?'

Not surprisingly, no one volunteered to take the leash because Kuma had acquired a fearsome reputation in the town. People were saying that he was a savage beast that attacked anyone that got in his way.

The fisherman walked under the jetty, looking for a place where Kuma could be tethered. He found a rusted spike protruding from a pile, and he hooked the leash's handle onto it. 'You won't be escaping this time,' he said, and then he turned to the crowd. 'Watch him until I get back, I will only be a few minutes.'

Kuma pulled at the leash, but it held firm. He looked to where the handle was hooked, but the spike was too high for him to reach. Escape was impossible. All he could do was to lie on the sand and watch the crowd as it gathered. He saw the traitorous old man arrive. 'You are a bad person that I will never trust again,' he woofed. Kuma's woofing startled the crowd.

'Stand back, everybody, he's turning vicious,' someone shouted.

'I've heard that mad dogs give you rabies,' came another shout.

A father and a little boy came as close as they dared. The boy held tight to his father's hand. Kuma stood up and wagged his tail. *At last, someone who likes me,'* he thought.

'Is that really the dog on the poster, daddy?' asked the boy.

'Yes, son, he's the leader of the Sheep Killers.'

'But he has weird ears. The dog on the poster is much better looking.'

'It's his disguise,' said the father, who always made things up when he did not know the answer.

'Wow, wait until I tell the kids at school that I have been this close to a killer,' said the boy.

The father cautioned, 'Don't get too close. Killers can be deceiving. He may look friendly, but that leash is all that stops him from attacking us.'

'What will happen to him, daddy?'

'They will shoot him I guess.'

The boy's eyes widened. 'Can we stay and watch.'

Kuma's tail dropped, and he lay back down on the sand. He no longer liked the little boy.

Meanwhile, the fisherman had arrived at the police station. It had taken him less than a minute, for nothing is ever far away in a small, country town. 'I claim the one hundred dollars reward for capture of the Sheep Killers' leader,' he announced. 'I have the prisoner tied to the jetty.'

'Hooray,' cried the constable. 'I shall make preparations for the evil hound to be taken into custody.' With that, he went out to the paddy wagon and removed a bale of hay and two bags of chook food. 'It's been a while since I've had a prisoner in there,' he said.

Kuma's fate seemed sealed, but that was not the case. Kitty had seen everything from the cliff top. She had seen Ralph's rescue, the fisherman's arrival, and Bruno's threatened attack. Kitty had laughed when she saw Kuma go by, barking like an idiot on the bow of the boat. However, she guessed that he would be in trouble once his ride was over. She had run along the beach trying to catch Kuma's attention, but he was too busy barking at the waves. She was now hiding under the jetty.

The paddy wagon pulled up and the constable got out. The fisherman was with him, and the two-man posse walked toward their captive. The constable was carrying a catch pole. 'Step aside, everybody, this is dangerous work,' he said.

The crowd separated and stood back, their tension eased because the law was now in charge. Some marvelled at the bravery of the constable who was about to grapple the dangerous felon. Kuma tried to hide behind the pile.

Suddenly, the crowd saw a flash of ginger as a small cat dashed from somewhere under the jetty. The cat scrambled up the pile that secured the leash. They saw the cat slip the leash off the spike. In a blink, the killer dog was free. Everyone scattered.

'Run, Kuma,' cried Kitty.

The two-man posse gasped as the two fugitives made a dash for freedom.

'I guess there goes my hundred bucks,' sighed the fisherman.

'My promotion too,' added the constable.

The fisherman felt a tug on his shirt. It was the young crabber. 'You owe me five bucks, and my dad wants his leash back.'

'But that dog has the leash,' protested the fisherman.

'That's not my dad's problem,' said the lad. 'Dad wants ten bucks if he doesn't get his leash back, and dad is the bouncer at the pub.'

The fisherman's day was going from bad to worse, but he was not giving up. He turned to the constable. 'We can chase him in my boat. Come on and bring that pole with you.'

'I can do better than that,' said the constable. He went back to the paddy wagon and grabbed his rifle.

20

THE TROUBLE MAGNET

The fugitives stopped running once they realised that no one was chasing them. They decided to walk along the beach and then leave it by going up the goat track. They did have the option of leaving the beach earlier by going up the gully, but they would then have to go through the scrub to get home. The scrub was the Sheep Killers' territory.

'I'm always having to get you out of trouble,' said Kitty. 'My life was much simpler before you came along.'

'You were living in a dump before I came along,' snorted Kuma.

'I know,' said Kitty, 'but I was safe there. Being around you is dangerous. You seem to attract trouble.'

Kuma pondered Kitty's words, for Kitty's lecture sounded familiar. 'You're right,' he said. 'My friend Jock told me that I was a trouble magnet. I think you would be safer without me.' He dropped his head.

'Don't be silly,' said Kitty. 'There is no such thing as a trouble magnet. If you were a trouble magnet, trouble would be following us right now.'

At that moment, they heard a boat. The fisherman and the constable were in hot pursuit, and their boat was fast gaining on them. Kitty had a sudden change of mind. *I was wrong,* she thought. *Kuma is a trouble magnet.* 'Run' she cried.

They ran for their lives, hoping to outpace their pursuers. The constable fired a shot, but he found it hard to aim from a bouncing boat. The fugitives continued to run, knowing the shooter's accuracy would improve once he got closer. They had to get off the beach. Ahead was the gully.

The constable fired again, and the bullet hit the beach, causing a puff of sand to rise next to Kitty. The constable's aim was getting better. 'Run for the gully,' cried Kitty. 'It's our only chance.'

They ran into the gully. Exhausted, they crouched behind a rock, but then the boat pulled onto the sand. The chase was on again.

'I know a bush where we can hide,' said Kitty.

They ran up the gully to a bush that was outside a fox's den. Kitty often used the bush to hide from the Sheep Killers, because the bush harboured a strong odour of fox musk. The odour would confuse the dogs' sense of smell and they could never find her.

They reached the bush and crouched in a hollow beneath it. They listened and could hear their pursuers coming toward them, but what they did not expect to hear was a voice coming from the other direction. 'So this is where you hide from us,' it said. They turned, and there was Bruno. With him were the Sheep Killers.

Bruno had witnessed everything from the safety of the cliff top and had seen his chance to ambush Kuma as he made his escape along the beach. He had hollered a chilling howl, which was his call to arms. The pack had come running, and he was now leading them down the gully. To find Kuma hiding before they reached the beach had been a surprise, but he did not realise that Kuma was running from the posse.

A butcherbird sang a warning. 'Humans are coming. Humans are coming.' Only then, did the Sheep Killers realise that Kuma had again drawn them into a trap. Panic arose as every dog looked for a place to hide. Bruno joined Kuma and Kitty under the bush, while the others scurried to find cover elsewhere.

Kitty's hiding place was big enough for her and Kuma, but everyone had to squish when Bruno arrived. Kitty crouched low beneath Kuma's tummy while Bruno was pressed hard against his body. With everyone so close and friendly, Kuma thought it only polite that he should say something nice. 'How is Spike getting on?' he whispered.

Bruno said nothing. He could not believe that Spike's attacker would actually flaunt the foul deed in his face.

'I didn't want to give him any trouble,' Kuma went on.

'You have been nothing but trouble ever since you arrived,' Bruno snarled.

'That's a coincidence,' said Kitty. 'I was just saying the same thing to Kuma, myself. Actually, Kuma is famous for his ability to attract trouble.'

Kuma's heart sank, for now even Kitty was telling people that he was a trouble magnet. 'I'm sorry,' he said. 'I only want to be friends with everyone.'

'No one would want you as a friend,' smirked Bruno, 'but in answer to your question, Spike is going to live, but your days are numbered.'

Kitty could see no point in trying to befriend Bruno, and she was annoyed that they were actually helping him to hide. Tomorrow, he would be out to get them again. She felt angry, and she could think of only one thing that would quell that anger. She sunk her teeth into Bruno's butt.

Bruno leapt out of the bush and let out a mighty yelp. The constable saw him and fired from the hip, the bullet whizzing past Bruno's nose. The hiding dogs saw Bruno's leap and thought he was showing his defiance of the law. They waited for his next inspirational action, but it did not provide the inspiration they expected. Follow me,' he barked, and he bolted for home.

The constable gasped as dogs appeared from everywhere. He did not know which to shoot first, for all were moving too fast. He let go a spray of bullets, but none found their mark. The dogs followed their leader with the fisherman and constable in hot pursuit. All were soon gone, and the gully returned to quiet.

In the nearby fox's den, a mother fox was woken from her slumber. She poked her sleeping husband in the ribs. 'Did you hear that?'

Father fox blinked his eyes and groaned. 'Did I hear what?'

'Outside—Hooligans—Gunshots. I don't know what this district is coming to.'

Father fox rolled over. 'Don't bother me now, dear, I need my sleep. I will deal with the matter when I get up at sunset. People should have more respect for us nocturnal animals.' He shut his eyes and put a paw over his ear.

With everyone gone, the coast was clear for Kuma and Kitty to return to the beach, but they kept hearing gunshots. 'I hope the dogs got away okay,' said Kuma.

Kitty shook her head. 'You are such a softie, Kuma. Those dogs wanted to kill you. How can you say that?'

Kuma could not explain why he felt no real malice toward the dogs, but he would have been pleased to know that the dogs did get away safely. The shots being heard were shots of frustration. The posse had found an innocent can and were taking it in turns to shoot it off a fence post. Meanwhile, the Sheep Killers had gathered in the scrub and were checking their casualties. All had escaped harm, but one.

'I think I might have been shot,' said Bruno.

'Where, boss?'

'Back there.' Bruno twisted his body in a futile attempt to inspect his own butt.

'Let me look, boss,'

'Well?'

'Sorry, boss. I can't see a bullet hole, but you do have an impressive set of teeth marks. Is there any chance that you might have sat on a cat?'

Sometime later, the fisherman and the constable returned to where they had left the boat. Unfortunately, no one had remembered to put out the anchor and the tide had come in. The boat had floated out to sea and was now a distant dot bobbing on the horizon. This was by far the worst day the fisherman could ever remember.

21

DINNER WITH THE KELPIES

The fugitives arrived back home and headed for the kennels. Kuma had not eaten since breakfast and was hoping that the kelpies had saved him some dinner. 'Got any leftovers?' he woofed as he bounded up from the dip.

'We have some for both of you,' said Seek.

Kuma's tail wagged as he headed for the food bowls, but then Destroy barked, 'Wait, we have to warn you about something.'

Kuma pretended that he did not hear, for the smell of food was making his mouth water, but Kitty stopped him in his tracks. 'Kuma, don't be rude. Sit down and listen to what the kelpies have to say.'
Kuma let out a snort and sat down.

'The Sheep Killers have a new leader,' barked Destroy.

'He's evil, and cunning, and has escaped custody twice,' added Seek.

'How do you know this?' asked Kuma.

'It's all over the bush telegraph,' said Seek. 'The kookaburra told us, and he heard it from the seagulls, and the seagulls know everything because seagulls see all.'

'Do they really see all?' asked Kuma.

'Not really,' said Seek, 'that is just something they like to say.'

'That's very interesting,' said Kuma. He got up and made a move toward the food bowls. Kitty stopped him. 'Don't be rude, Kuma. The kelpies haven't finished their story.'

'It's a stupid story,' whispered Kuma. 'We both know that Bruno is the leader of the Sheep Killers. The seagulls tell lies.'

'You don't like seagulls, do you?' laughed Kitty.

'No,' snorted Kuma. He took a step toward the food bowls, but then Destroy stood in his way.

'We all have to watch out for the new leader,' he barked. 'They say he is dangerous and no one should stand in his way. He was last seen with a red leash hanging from his collar.'

Seek gave Destroy a nudge and took him aside. He whispered in Destroy's ear, 'Is that a red leash hanging from Kuma's collar?'

Destroy looked at Kuma and tilted his head. Shock, horror, Kuma had a red leash hanging from his collar. 'You're right,' he said. 'We have to report this to MacLeod at once.'

'Wait,' said Seek. 'We must be careful that Kuma doesn't get suspicious. The kookaburra said that he is dangerous. I think we should warn Kitty first.'

However, Kitty had already realised that Kuma's red leash had become a problem. She was whispering in Kuma's ear. 'I think they have seen your red leash.'

'It doesn't look red to me,' said Kuma.

'Kuma, dogs are colour-blind. You don't know what red is.'

Kuma looked at the kelpies. 'Good, well neither do they.'

'You're right,' said Kitty, and she went into damage control. 'What does everyone think of Kuma's green leash?' she said.

'Are you sure that it's not red?' asked Destroy.

'No, it's green, definitely green. I think green goes well with Kuma's fur, don't you?'

Both kelpies agreed that green did look good on Kuma. With that settled, Kuma walked once more toward the food, but with three more paces to go, Seek barked, 'Wait.'

'What now?' said Kuma.

'We have to tell you about our exciting day.'

Kuma took another step forward, but Kitty stopped him. 'Kuma, remember your manners. The kelpies want to tell you about their exciting day.'

Kuma sat down. 'How come you don't seem as hungry as I am?' he whispered.

'I ate a mouse.'

'When?'

'While I was waiting for you under the jetty.'

'You didn't offer me any.'

'Kuma, it was a mouse, not a horse. You will get to eat once the kelpies tell their story.'

Kuma sighed. He would do his best to listen, but the food bowls were a big distraction. *I'm sure that's a chicken wing in that bowl,* he thought.

Seek began. 'You will never guess what we saw today.'

'A chicken wing,' said Kuma.

'Kuma, pay attention and stop thinking about food,' growled Kitty.

'Okay,' Kuma sighed. He rested his chin on his paws.

Seek continued. 'I saw a rabbit, and I chased it.'

'I chased a rabbit too,' added Destroy.

'Oh, that's right,' said Seek. 'We were chasing two rabbits.'

Destroy nodded, and then Seek went on with the story. 'Suddenly, there was a third rabbit.'

'A third rabbit,' said Kitty. 'That must have been amazing.'

Kuma was not impressed with Kitty interrupting. He was in a hurry for the boring story to end so that he could eat.

Destroy took up the telling of the tale. 'It was the most incredible rabbit we have ever seen.'

'It was white,' said Seek. 'Imagine that, a white rabbit on our farm.'

'Fantastic,' said Kuma. He got up and took another step toward the food.

'But then something else happened,' said Destroy. Kuma sat down again. 'On the way back, I bailed up a sleepy lizard. I thought it was a snake at first, but they say that sleepy lizards can be just as dangerous.'

'I know,' said Kuma, who had no idea what a sleepy lizard even looked like.

Kuma went to get up again but Destroy had more to say. 'I'm sorry, Kuma. We are being rude. We have been telling you about our exciting day, but we haven't asked you anything about yours. How has your day been?'

Kuma thought for a moment. He had saved the lambs, thrown Spike off a cliff, befriended a snake, saved a seal, been for a boat ride, been captured by the law, escaped from the law, and had rubbed shoulders with Bruno. There was no way that he was going to waste time telling them any of that. He wanted to eat. 'We just went to the beach,' he said.

'That sounds nice,' said Destroy.

'It was,' blurted Kuma, who could wait no longer and had begun to hoover into Seek's leftovers. Kitty made a dash to the other bowl, knowing that she would have to be quick, or she would miss out altogether.

Destroy gave Seek a smug glance. 'Why are our lives so much more exciting that other people's?' he asked.

'I don't know,' said Seek. 'I guess we are just more adventurous.'

Kitty glared at Kuma. 'Don't you dare roll your eyes,' she whispered.

22

LEAVE TOWN OR ELSE

Kuma and Kitty returned to the Volkswagen and found the sheep grazing nearby. The kelpies had told them to stay close to the car at night so that Kuma could guard them. Kuma was soon stretched out on the back seat, ready for a good night's sleep, but Kitty was about to give him a lecture.

'You behaved very badly tonight,' she said. 'Seek and Destroy are my friends, but you embarrassed me. All you wanted to do was eat.'

'I was hungry,' pleaded Kuma.

'That's no excuse. I don't behave badly to your friends.'

'Sorry,' said Kuma. 'I will try to do better next time.'

Kuma closed his eyes but then wondered if Kitty was being fair. *Kitty doesn't have to worry about upsetting my friends because I have no friends of my own,* he thought. *I only know her friends.* He was about to inform her of this fact when he realised that he was wrong. He had just made a friend called Simon who was living downstairs. Kuma had forgotten to say goodnight to his new friend.

'Are you under the car, Simon?' he called.

'Yes,' came a voice from below.

Kitty leapt through the space, which once housed the windscreen. With a loud clunk, she landed on the front bonnet. 'There's a snake under the bed,' she screamed.

'No there isn't,' said Kuma. 'Simon is under the car, not the bed.'

'Same thing.'

'No it isn't.'

'Yes it is.'

'Simon, it's not the same thing, is it?'

'No.'

'See, Kitty, it's not the same thing. I bet Simon would much rather be sleeping up here where we are.'

'Yes please,' called Simon.

'NO!' screamed Kitty. 'I am not sleeping in the same room as a snake.'

Kuma frowned. 'But, Kitty, you are not being polite to my new friend.'

'Simon doesn't count.'

Kuma sighed, 'Sorry Simon, but Kitty said that you have to stay where you are.'

'That's okay,' he replied. 'Cats make me nervous anyway.'

Kitty came back inside, and Kuma closed his eyes. He had just learnt something new about his feline friend. She had double standards.

Kuma was asleep when two dogs, one large and one small, came to their door later that night. The small dog let out a sharp yap and everyone woke up. 'What was that?' baaed the sheep. Kuma opened his eyes. He hated being woken from peaceful slumber. It made him grumpy.

'We are Bruno's messengers, and we have a message for the trouble magnet,' barked the big dog.

Kuma resented the label of trouble magnet, but he was finding it hard to argue otherwise. It was the middle of the night and two of Bruno's henchmen were standing at his door. Trouble had found him again.

'What's the message?' Kuma snapped.

'Tell him, Jasper.'

Jasper hopped onto the driver's seat and Kitty recognised him at once. 'Jasper, what are you doing with the Sheep Killers? You're too small to kill sheep.' Jasper had been a neighbour's dog, but he had mysteriously left home.

'Hello, Kitty,' said Jasper. 'I'm their new messenger boy. They said that they would bite my ears off if I didn't join them. Can you imagine how ugly a dog would look with deformed ears?'

'I have no idea,' said Kitty, but Kuma said nothing. Jasper's question had left him thinking, *I hate Jasper.*

'Stop fraternizing with the enemy, Jasper,' growled the big dog. He threw Jasper out of the car and stood with his front paws on the driver's seat. 'Bruno says that if you are here in the morning, you are dead meat, so get out of town now.'

'Why isn't Bruno telling me this himself?' grumped Kuma.

The dog gave careful thought before answering. 'The boss never raids at night. He leaves the night raids to Spike, but Spike is unwell at the moment.'

'They say that Bruno is afraid of the dark,' yapped Jasper.

'Quiet, Jasper,' said the big dog. 'If the boss ever hears you say that, you will have more than your ears missing.'

Kuma felt cranky, and he was half-asleep, which can be a dangerous combination. 'Tell Bruno to come here and I will have it out with him, dog-to-dog,' he growled.

Oh no, that's not a good idea, thought Kitty.

'That will be your funeral,' laughed the big dog.

The two dogs left and there was silence for a while, but then Kuma said, 'Who would have thought that a big dog like Bruno would be afraid of the dark.'

'It's certainly hard to imagine,' said Kitty. She flicked her eyes skyward and shook her head, but fortunately, it was too dark for Kuma to see her.

23

THE FINAL SHOWDOWN

Kuma looked out at daybreak, but Bruno was nowhere to be seen. Beatrice and Roger were standing at the cliff top, planning another day of exploration. Everything appeared peaceful, and so Kuma suggested that he and Kitty go for a breakfast of kelpie leftovers.

The two arrived at the kennels where they heard again the boring stories about the white rabbit and the sleepy lizard. This time, Kuma listened patiently, for he did not want another lecture from Kitty. Once the tales had been told, Kuma scoffed his breakfast. Kitty was pleased by his better behaviour this time, but he still needed to improve his table manners. *I must teach him to eat more slowly,* she thought.

Kuma gulped down his last mouthful just as the kookaburra arrived. He had bad news. Bruno and his boys were back at the Volkswagen, and the lambs were in trouble. Kuma and Kitty raced for home, leaving the kelpies to raise the alarm.

Kuma was first back, and he found Bruno standing at the top of the goat track. The lambs were trapped on the ledge, and the Sheep Killers were gathered on the beach. 'Go on down, little sheep,' said Bruno. 'Those nice doggies on the beach want to play with you.'

'Stay where you are,' barked Kuma.

Bruno spun around. 'I thought you had done the smart thing and left,' he growled.

'Never,' said Kuma.

'So, you want your dog-to-dog settlement, do you?'

I think I did say something about a dog-to-dog settlement, thought Kuma, but he could not be held responsible for anything he had said when half-asleep.

Bruno bared his fangs. The lambs could wait. He leapt at Kuma and the two dogs locked jaws. They rolled to within centimetres of going over the cliff and then common sense prevailed. If they fell together, neither would be the winner. The contest would end as a draw, decided under the most unfortunate of circumstances. They broke apart and Kuma scrambled toward the Volkswagen. 'Go find your mum,' he called to the lambs, but they were too frightened to move. Kitty arrived and ran down the goat track. It would be up to her to rescue the lambs.

The dogfight continued by the Volkswagen as the dogs on the beach listened from below. They could not see the fight, but they cheered every snarl and growl. They were waiting for the painful yelp that would foreshadow Kuma's demise. Victory to the Sheep Killers seemed certain, but then help arrived. Troy and the kelpies came running from the farmhouse.

Troy ignored the fighting dogs, for he could hear the lambs bleating on the cliff face. He scrambled down the goat track to rescue them. At that moment, Kuma let out a yelp. Bruno had sunk his teeth into the back of his neck and was not letting go. Kuma was helpless. He collapsed to the ground.

Bruno released his grip, satisfied that the bite had done its job. He returned to the top of the goat track where he was surprised to find a group of four now standing on the ledge, and one was a human. He would have to deal with the human first.

Bruno fixed an evil glare on Troy, which caused Beatrice to panic. Troy reached out a hand to steady her. However, his sudden action caused him to slip. He felt his body slide over the ledge, but just in time, he grabbed hold of a protruding rock. He hung on with both hands, but the rock could break away at any moment.

Troy's dilemma simplified Bruno's task. Lambs, cats, and humans were all the same to him. Dogs were the only species who had a life worth preserving. Humans were no better than the rest, but they were trickier to deal with. However, this one would be easy.

Kitty saw the danger, but she was not giving up without a fight. She leapt at Bruno, determined to scratch his eyes out. She sunk her claws into his forehead, but Bruno grabbed her by the tail and flung back his head. The dogs on the beach cheered as Kitty fell through the air.

The way was now clear for Bruno to deal with Troy. A mere nip on the fingers would see him plunge. He stood over his victim, so close that Troy could smell his foul breath. All hope seemed lost, but then there came a woof. Kuma had dragged himself to the top of the goat track.

'You haven't finished him off, boss,' came a bark from the beach.

Bruno looked at the bullmastiff staring him down. Such defiance required a quick response.

Kuma had no fight left in him, but he was still capable of luring Bruno away from his victims. He dragged himself into the long grass and Bruno followed. The dogs on the beach listened from below.

Bruno glared at Kuma as he lay helpless. 'Now you learn what happens to dogs who defy my authority,' he snarled. He went to lunge at the defenceless Kuma, but then froze. He looked down and gasped. The thing he feared most in the world was at his feet. 'S-snake,' he stammered.

Simon sank his fangs into Bruno's leg. Bruno gave a terrified yelp. The dogs on the beach looked at each other. 'That sounds like Bruno,' said one.

'Ridiculous,' said another.

However, they soon saw that the first dog was correct, for Bruno came to the cliff top. 'I think I'm dying,' he howled, and then he staggered from their sight.

'It looks like he's taking the short way home,' said one of the pack. 'Best we head back along the beach.' The dogs left, not realising that more was still happening behind them.

For thousands of years, people have marvelled at the falling ability of cats. A falling cat always lands on its feet, and a cat can walk away from a fall that most creatures would find fatal. The pack's attention had been solely on Bruno, and no one took notice of a small splash that happened behind them.

Bruno's treatment of Kitty had been so forceful, that she had been thrown over the beach and into the water. This rather undignified treatment had taught her two things. She was good at falling but hated to swim. Had the pack turned around, they would have seen a bruised and sodden Kitty dragging herself ashore.

Troy emerged at the top of the cliff with a lamb under each arm. At the same time, MacLeod arrived in the truck. 'The dogs were trying to kill the lambs,' Troy yelled.

MacLeod grabbed his rifle and looked about. At first, he saw no dogs, but then he saw their leader. The bullmastiff, with a price on his head, was lying in the long grass and was about to attack Troy. He raised his rifle and took aim. 'Stand back, Troy,' he yelled, 'there's a dog right by you, and I'm going to shoot it.'

Troy saw Kuma lying in the grass. 'STOP, DAD. THAT DOG SAVED MY LIFE!' He dropped the lambs to the ground and waved his hands in the air.

The lambs raced over to Kuma. 'Are you alright, Kuma?' asked Beatrice.

'I think so,' Kuma mumbled, 'but you should not have been on that ledge.' Kuma could barely open his eyes.

'But we had to be there,' explained Beatrice. 'That's our lookout, and you asked us to look out for the trawler.'

Kuma suddenly felt that everything had been his fault. His thoughtlessness had put the lambs in danger. He drew in a breath to apologise, but Beatrice had not finished. 'And guess what?' she said. 'The trawler has come back. We were coming to tell you that when the dog stopped us.'

Kuma raised his head and tried to get to his feet. He wanted to see the trawler for himself, but he was too weak to move.

24

A HOME AT LAST

Kuma lay on his side, wondering which part of him hurt the least. Simon slithered as close as he dared, for he had to stay out of sight. 'Are you all right, Kuma?' he whispered.

Kuma gave his reptile friend a painful nod. 'I will be okay in a few days, thanks, Simon, but you need to hide. They don't realise that it was you who just saved us all.'

'My pleasure,' said Simon. He slithered away and few would ever know of the great service he had performed that day. Such is the life of a snake.

MacLeod gently lifted Kuma and Kitty onto the back of the truck, and the kelpies tried to join them. 'Get down, dogs, you can walk home,' growled MacLeod.

Seek looked at Destroy. 'Can you believe that? We were the heroes who raised the alarm, but we don't get a ride.'

'We saved them all,' said Destroy, 'but where's the gratitude?'

They both agreed that life was unfair.

Back at the farmhouse, the injured heroes were given warm beds in the laundry. MacLeod called the vet, and all wounds were cleaned and dressed. Soothing medicine was prescribed, and Kuma took his like a man. However, Kitty fought to the bitter end. It took the combined effort of both vet and farmer to force her tablet down.

'The bullmastiff is going to have scars,' said the vet, 'but the pussycat will be back catching mice in no time.'

Great, thought Kuma. *Now I have scars to go with my funny ears. Everyone will laugh at me.*

Kitty was equally unimpressed. *Pussycat,* she thought. *I'm not a pussycat. I'm a feline warrior, mistress of the bush.*

The two patients spent a pain free night thanks to the vet's soothing medicine. Kitty slept peacefully, but Kuma's thoughts made him restless. He would doze a little and then be awake. The moon was shining through the laundry window, and he could see Kitty in her bed under the wash-trough. He was lying on his Kuma-sized bed alongside the washing machine.

Beatrice had said that the trawler was back, and Kuma's plan had been to run to the jetty when it returned. He was going to bark, Jason would hear him, come out, grab his collar, and drag him back onto the trawler. Unfortunately, his injuries now prevented that from happening, but that was not the problem that was keeping him awake. *Do I really want to leave?* he wondered. He loved his new life with Kitty, but would people let him stay?

Next morning, the two patients were served breakfast in bed. Kitty was almost back to her normal self, and she was about to go for a walk when they heard a voice outside. Kuma thought that he recognised the voice, but it was hard for him to move.

'Do you know who that is?' he asked Kitty.

'That man comes here all the time,' she said. 'He comes from the trawler to exchange fish for the things we grow on the farm.'

Kuma now understood why the food on the trawler was so nice. 'He's the skipper of Jason's trawler,' Kuma said.

Then Kuma heard another voice. 'Come here you idiot, or I will leave you behind next time.'

Kuma knew that voice too, and his heart jumped. Jason was outside, and he was calling someone an idiot. Kuma tried to stagger to the door, but the vet's medicine had made him wobbly. He let out a woof, but his woof was too feeble for Jason to hear.

'Who is he calling an idiot?' Kuma asked.

'I will check,' said Kitty.

Kitty left, but she was no sooner gone before Kuma heard a yap. Next, he heard a sharp meow, a yelp, a scurry, a thump on a fence, and then a bucket rolling over. Kitty came flying through the door and leapt on top of the washing machine. A small dog came hurtling through the door behind her.

'Get lost you mangy mongrel,' hissed Kitty, as she bared her claws.

The dog came to a sudden halt. He looked at Kitty, and then he looked at Kuma.

Kuma stared at their unexpected visitor. 'Jock! Is that you?' he said.

The Scottish Terrier wagged his tail. 'Kuma, my wayward wanderer. Aye, laddie, tis me. So, this is where your voyage took you.'

'Is he a friend of yours,' growled Kitty.

'This is my friend Jock. The one I'm always telling you about.'

'Now I know where you get your bad manners from,' Kitty scoffed.

Kuma looked at Jock. 'Please don't hurt Kitty. She is my friend.'

Jock sighed. 'You are such a softie, laddie. Have I taught you nothing? What fun does life have for a dog if he can't chase a cat?'

'Please,' pleaded Kuma.

Jock looked at the cat glaring down from the washing machine. 'Come on down, lassie. Any friend of Kuma is a friend of mine.'

Kitty hopped to the floor, but she was ready to rip Jock apart should he make one false move. Kuma told them that they had to be friends, and then he asked Jock how he came to be there.

'Looking for you, laddie,' said Jock. 'Jason was never going to find you on his own, and so I came along to help.'

'He asked for your help?' queried Kuma.

'Sort of,' said Jock. 'I just happened to hop on board, and he said I could stay.'

'But Jock, you hate being at sea.'

'Maybe I misjudged it a bit that first time,' Jock shrugged. 'but I had to help find you, laddie. It was my fault that you got stuck on the trawler in the first place, and strays have to stick together.'

Jock was right. Strays did have to stick together. It was then that Kuma realised his reason for feeling some empathy for the Sheep Killers, for they were strays as well, but they had come under the influence of an evil leader.

Kuma told Jock about his job, and about the Volkswagen with its ocean view.

'Kuma's home is my home too,' said Kitty.

Jock frowned. 'You have a cat, the sworn enemy of dogs, and she is your housekeeper. What is this world coming to?'

'Careful what you say about Kitty,' warned Kuma. 'Kitty is my friend, not my housekeeper, and she has fought a dog ten times your size.'

However, Jock's arrival had further complicated Kuma's dilemma. He liked living on the farm with Kitty, but Jock had suffered a sea voyage to bring him home. *But where is my home?* Kuma wondered. 'Thank you, Jock, for braving the seas to find me,' he said.

Jock laughed, 'Actually, laddie, had it not been for you, I would never have ventured to sea for a second time, and would never have discovered the joy that comes from plying the waves. The feeling you get when you stand at the bow is like nothing I have ever known. You should try it.'

Kuma felt something stir inside. 'The bow ploughs into the wave,' he said.

'That's right,' said Jock, his tail wagging.

'And then it lifts.'

Jock nodded.

'And then it crashes back down.'

Jock nodded again.

'You bark as the spray balloons out.'

'You've done it,' said Jock.

'I love it!' said Kuma.

So do I,' said Jock.

Kitty shook her head. The things that could amuse a dog were things she would never understand.

It was then that Jason came into the laundry. He was looking for Jock and was not expecting to find Kuma.

'I've found him,' woofed Jock.

Jason stood stunned, and then he smiled. He knelt and gave Kuma a pat. 'What have you done to yourself, you poor fella?'

MacLeod poked his head through the door. 'He'll be right soon enough. That dog is a hero. By this time tomorrow, the whole district will be singing his praises. The vet is telling everyone his story.'

Jason told MacLeod about the dogcatcher and how Kuma came to be on the trawler. MacLeod then told Jason about Kuma's bravery, and that he would like to keep Kuma as a guard dog.

'I think Kuma would like that,' said Jason, 'and I reckon Jock wants to sign on as trawler crew. If he does that, he can visit Kuma whenever we are in port.'

The dogs were listening, and Jock's tail wagged. Kuma's tail tried to do the same, but it could only manage a feeble twitch. However, both dogs were happy. Two strays had found a home.

In the weeks that followed, Kuma made a full recovery. He had become the canine celebrity and could walk through town without a leash. Everyone wanted to pat him, and the butcher would give him a treat whenever he passed the shop. Even the treacherous old man wanted to give him a pat, but Kuma would always turn and walk away.

Kitty paid a visit to the neighbours and discovered that Jasper had moved back home. He told her that no one saw Bruno after that morning, and that Spike no longer wanted to lead the pack on raids. With no leaders, the gang had broken up. Some went back home, while others went south to hunt kangaroos. Spike was one of those who went home.

25

FULL CIRCLE

Life on a farm goes in a circle. There is a time to sow, a time to reap, a time to work, and a time to relax. The farmers all looked forward to that time for relaxation, for that was when the town would host its annual farmers' field day. Farmers would come from the surrounding districts to meet with other farmers. They would inspect new machinery, exchange ideas, and bring their prized animals for showing. MacLeod and Troy always went to the field days, but they never took a prize animal to show. They only took the kelpies who competed in the sheep dog trials, but the kelpies were yet to win a prize.

The annual field day had come around again, and as always, MacLeod and Troy headed there in the truck. The kelpies were on the back, but this time, they had Kuma with them. Kitty had also managed to hitch a ride in the cabin, for everywhere Kuma went, she wanted to go too. The kelpies were wondering why Kuma and Kitty were with them.

'Why are you going to the field day?' said Seek. 'You're not a farm animal.'

'What's a field day?' Kuma asked.

'See, that proves my point,' came the reply. 'You don't even know what a field day is.'

Destroy agreed, but Kuma did not bother to answer. He lived on a farm, and so he was a farm animal.

MacLeod parked the truck alongside the many other vehicles that were lined up in the field day car park. The kelpies were then taken to the sheep dog area while Troy took Kuma to the animal shed. The animal shed was full of pens and cages, and Kuma was left in one of them. Kitty stayed in the carpark, sound asleep on the back of the truck.

Surprisingly, Kuma saw that the cages around him each held a perfectly groomed bullmastiff. He lay on the floor and tried to cover his ears, feeling ashamed to show them in such impressive company. However, the dog in the cage next door began a conversation.

'Hello,' said the dog. 'My name is Ulysses, and I once had a brother with an ear like yours.'

The other dogs, who were all rather bored, began to listen.

'Did you also have a sister called Portia?' Kuma asked.

'I did,' said Ulysses, 'but how do you know?'

'I think you two might be related,' came a sarcastic comment from one of those listening.

Ulysses looked at Kuma. 'You sound like Kuma, but Kuma was chubby, and you look like an athlete.'

'An active life on a farm can do that to a fella,' said Kuma.

Ulysses tilted his head. 'But how come you have two weird ears? The last time I saw you, you only had one.'

'Oh that,' said Kuma. 'That's a bullet wound. My friend tells me that it makes me look like a pirate.'

A collective wow went through those listening. Everyone was impressed. None of them could boast that they had a bullet wound.

'What about your other scars?' asked Ulysses.

'That's just more battle damage,' Kuma shrugged, 'but why are you all here?'

'I'm not sure,' said Ulysses. 'I think they are having a special showing of bullmastiffs, but I don't know why.'

The day passed slowly for the dogs in the cages, despite there being many visitors. It seemed that most had come to see the dog with the weird ears, but one visitor did come to see Ulysses. That visitor was the man who had sold Ulysses and then dumped Kuma in the street. He recognised Kuma by his ear and was shocked to realise that Kuma was the famous dog many had come to see. Farmers were saying how they would have liked to own a dog like Kuma. *I could have sold him for a fortune,* thought the man. Ulysses greeted the man with a woof, but Kuma ignored him.

Ulysses was surprised by Kuma's rudeness to the man who had once owned them, for he did not know that Kuma had been dumped.

Kuma told the story.

'You must hate that man,' said Ulysses.

'I don't know,' said Kuma. 'If he hadn't dumped me, I would not be having the life that I now have.'

Kuma then told of his adventures, from the day he first met Jock until his appointment as guardian of the sheep. The other dogs listened in awe. One said, 'I wish I had a life like yours. I just get taken from show to show and sit in a cage all day.'

'That's all any of us do,' said Ulysses. 'I wish I had been born with an odd ear. Perhaps then, I would be having a great life too. At that point, the bullmastiffs were taken to a special arena, but Kuma was left behind. A short while later, they returned. 'Where have you all been?' Kuma asked.

Ulysses sighed. 'It appears farmers have all become interested in bullmastiffs and are having a special event for them this year.

'What sort of event?'

'Just another boring dog-show for bullmastiffs,' said Ulysses. 'Thank goodness it's over. I've been wanting to scratch my ear all day but couldn't because it would ruffle my fur.'

Kuma was impressed that Ulysses had become a show dog, and his sense of family pride prompted him to ask, 'Who won?'

'I did,' said Ulysses.

'Congratulations,' said Kuma.

Ulysses shrugged. 'Thanks, but it's no big deal. I've won lots of blue ribbons, but I would swap them all for a life like yours. Being allowed to scratch yourself once the event is over is actually the highlight of a show dog's day.' He scratched his ear once more.

The field day was coming to an end with only the most sought-after award still to be announced. The cup for the farm's most valuable animal was traditionally awarded at the end of the day. Horatio, the bull, had won it for the past two years, for he had been a champion at the state's Royal Show. This year, he was champion again. People began heading for their cars, for all knew what the result would be. They listened to the announcer's preamble and then they heard him say, 'This year, we have two winners, Kuma and Kitty. This brave pair put their own lives on the line to save one of our local lads, and Kuma is now a steadfast guardian of the sheep.'

There was loud applause and people returned to gather around the podium. Troy went up and accepted two silver bowls.

Kuma heard the announcement but had no idea what was happening. His day had been special for other reasons. He had met his brother and seen the man who had once dumped him. Strangely, he held no hard feelings, for he had found his own place in the world, and he envied no one.

In real life, Kuma and Kitty were two inseparable friends who lived in the Adelaide Hills. This imagined story has them meeting in a rubbish dump, but their true-life meeting was just as dramatic. This poem tells how they met on a Christmas Eve some years ago.

A CHRISTMAS TAIL

Visitors to the farmhouse,
Would stop at the steel fenced pen,
For there in lived a monster,
With the strength of many men.
No human bone existed,
That the creature could not crunch.
Those massive paws, those crushing jaws,
Could have a man for lunch.

But the mastiff barely moved,
When visitors ushered by.
None would see his gentle heart,
Or sadness in his eye.
For destiny had ordained him,
A misfit for a farm.
He knew not why none came near,
He meant them all no harm.

Confined by sturdy fences,
For neighbours all had doubt.
Those unthinkable consequences,
Should ever he break out.
His long and lonely hours,
Held boredom with no end.
Salvation seemed so far away,
He longed for just one friend.

A Dog on the Run

A friend to share his feelings,
A soul mate by his side.
A friend that understood him,
That wouldn't run and hide.
When either be in trouble,
The other would defend.
Someone pleased to see him,
He longed for such a friend.

Then on the eve of Christmas Day,
An evil deed played out.
A car stopped by the roadside,
When no one was about.
The driver's window opened,
And then without a sound,
A little ginger kitten,
Was dropped roughly to the ground.

The car drove off in a cloud of dust,
The kitten watched it go.
Shaking both from fear and cold,
In a place she did not know.
The trees swayed all around her,
'Twas a dark and chilly night.
Then flickering through the moving shapes,
The kitten saw a light.

Though frightened, cold, and hungry,
Overwhelmed by all about.
Curiosity demanded,
She check the strange light out.
She crept toward its glimmer,
'Til a barrier crossed her trail.
From there she viewed a window,
Through the bars of a monster's jail.

Not knowing these bars had purpose,
She easily passed them by.
For her nostrils caught a whiff of food,
And a large bowl caught her eye.
Her hunger dragged her to it,
Behold she found a feast.
Enough to feed fifty cats,
Or perhaps one very large beast.

In an instant she was eating,
But the meal did barely begin.
When a large wet smelly object,
Pushed her headfirst in.
A huge and sloppy tongue
Then licked her north to south,
But most frightening of all,
It hung from a massive mouth.

As quick as a flash the kitten sprang,
As only a kitten can.
To be part of a monster's meal,
Was not the kitten's plan.
Her little brain now spinning,
One life had met its fate,
And only clever planning,
Would save her other eight.

A Dog on the Run

But the plans we make in haste,
Are never best of all,
And the ginger ball of lightning,
Just went thud into a wall.
Her escape plan was in shambles,
The way out hard to see,
The windowsill the only option,
This was her plan B.

The beast watched on in wonder,
This fur ball in a flurry.
Her gymnastics most impressive,
Though spoilt by the hurry.
The scramble up the wall,
The balance on the sill,
A performance so amazing,
In awe he stood stock-still.

With the monster safe below her,
But no place left to go.
The kitten turned and there behind,
Was a cat she did not know.
But the ally though the window,
Gave a disappointing clue,
Snarls and nasty hissing,
This was enemy number two.

Glass separated one foe,
A large drop did the other.
The kitten seemed to find herself,
In a spot of bother.
Stuck on a narrow windowsill,
Heart pounding from her fright,
A watchful monster waiting,
She settled for the night.

That monster had her measure,
Escape a hopeless feat,
But then a strange thing happened,
Each time their eyes would meet.
The monster's tail would twitch,
A cat's sign to stay away.
But a dog has different meaning,
It means they want to play.

Now how the kitten figured it,
No one ever knew,
But the message of the tail,
Eventually got through.
And a literal leap of faith,
Saw that kitten on the ground,
And the tail madly wagging,
On a very happy hound.

The sun rose crisp that Christmas morn,
And softly spread its light,
And from the house came sounds of joy,
And screams of great delight.
Santa's magic filled little hearts,
His gifts had brought great cheer.
To think that he and reindeer too
That night had been so near.

Now little minds do think a lot,
So often they ask why.
But never had they questioned once,
How sleigh and reindeer fly.
But now they had a question,
How did Santa come and go?
How did they all get past the dog?
Their parents did not know.

A Dog on the Run

Some things occur in childhood,
That forever with us stay,
And the children keep forever,
Their surprise that Christmas Day.
When they ran concerned to that monster's pen,
What was wrong? they took a peep.
And there they found their guard dog lay,
With a kitten, sound asleep.

Speculation quickly followed,
Perhaps no one ever knew,
That in certain situations,
Santa calls on animals too.
What other explanation,
Could there ever be,
The kitten was Santa's gift,
That anyone could see.

But the farmyard life is tough,
As all farm creatures know.
You either have a useful task,
Or you have to go.
It was shortly that same morning,
The farmer had his say.
"We already have a cat,
That kitten cannot stay."

But yet another plan went wrong,
For the farmer met his match.
No matter how hard he tried,
That kitten he could not catch.
For the kitten stayed by the mastiff's side,
That mastiff sensed her fear,
And like a statue stood his ground,
And let nobody near.

Robert Kingsley Hawes

Years went by on the little farm,
That had a steel fenced pen.
But now two happy creatures shared,
What had been a lonely den.
And the mastiff's manner warmed many hearts,
Neighbours even tipped their hat,
To the only dog they ever knew,
To own and love a cat.